Eagle's Nest
Bears And Eagles Seven

Determination Against All Odds
R.P. Wollbaum

Chapter One

Rick had spent the first week of his leave at home. Resting up and visiting with his parents, grandparents and sister. His nephew was now the age when Rick began to consider little people as real people. He was involved in soccer, baseball, and football. He was tall and skinny and more than a little clumsy, but what he lacked in coordination, he made up for in determination and spirit. Not having his own father was not a problem, he had about a hundred fathers, each of them devoted to the little tyke.

"Liz, I think the little monster is getting spoiled," Rick said one day. "Everyone dotes on his every wish and think it's cute when he misbehaves."

"Not by me he isn't," Elizabeth said.

"Ya, I know, but everyone else is scared to say anything for fear of upsetting you. Even his Grandparents don't do anything unless it is really bad."

"I don't believe that Gadget," Elizabeth said.

"When was the last time you came to one of his games?" Rick asked. "I plan on going to the one today."

"I can't, I have a Roads planning meeting today."

"Your loss Liz. I'll see you later."

Rick was early for the game. He helped the volunteer umpire set up the bases and the chalk lines and as the coaches and the teams started to arrive, Rick climbed to the back of the bleachers, pulled an almost cool coke out of his pocket and watched. While Rudys team mates were respectful, none of them joked around with Rudy like they did with each other. Much of the time they tried to avoid him. It started during warm ups. Rudy kept haranguing those who made the smallest mistakes and blamed others for his own. This is not going to turn out well, Rick thought.

By the second inning, the team was down five runs to none and Rudy was disrupting the team with his rantings so badly that they lost all cohesion and will to play. Taking matters into his own hands, Rick walked down to the bench as the team came off the field for their turn at Bat.

"Hey coach, got a second?" Rick said.

"Bench Rudy," Rick said when the coach came over. "He's killing you guys."

"Can't do that. He's the Countesses son," the coach said.

"Well I am the Countess' brother and I'm telling you to bench him. If you don't I will pull him from the game myself. But I think it will be a valuable lesson for him to sit out the rest of this game and that you only play him at the beginning of each game for his minimum amount of innings until he improves his attitude and skill level."

"You Warrant Bekenbaum?" the coach asked.

"Von Hoaedle, you sit the rest of the game out," the coach said after Rick nodded.

Rudy was so shocked he didn't notice Rick climb back up to the stands. He threw his glove under the bench and sat glaring for the rest of the game, which his team rallied from behind and won. The first win of the year. The rest of the team celebrated the victory with high fives and ran out to shake hands with the losers, except for Rudy, who stayed sullenly on the bench pouting.

"I'll take him home coach," Rick said. "Come on nephew, you're with me."

Rick listened to Rudy rant and rave about how he had been mistreated all the way to the plush home he and his mother shared. Ricks old truck had barely come to a stop, when Rudy flung himself out the door and stomped his way into the house.

"Mom, you fire that stupid coach. He doesn't know what he is doing. He benched me in the second. He's always picking on me. It's not fair!"

Rick walked into the kitchen to see Rudy stomping his feet and grabbed him by the uniform collar, lifting him off the ground, so that they were eye ball to eye ball.

"Your coach didn't pull you," Rick said. "I did. You embarrassed me out there. You disrespected your coach and your teammates. Your behaviour discredits me, your mother and your father's memory. I am ashamed to be related to you."

"You let him talk to you like that Liz?" Rick said, shifting his gaze to his sister. "Mom would have kicked my ass all the way down the street for acting like this. Do you think you are doing him any favours codling him like this? He is already a little tyrant. He will never be a leader or even a good team member at this rate. Nobody wants to have anything to do with him and if you weren't the Countess, he would get his ass kicked every day at school. From what I can see young man, you will never be the man your father was."

Rick put Rudy back on the floor, nodded at his sister and walked out.

"Waste of a fantastic gene pool," he muttered under his breath and drove the twelve kilometres home.

The next day, Rick was in his workshop studying some intelligence reports. It would seem that the Pakistanis were training all of these Muslim extremist groups in camps all around Afghanistan. The Afghan government supported them and the camps were funded by wealthy Saudis. Something would have to be done about this soon, as these groups were being linked to a large number of terrorist activities around the world. But every time it was brought up at the UN Security Council, any reprisal actions were always vetoed by the Russians and the Chinese.

Ricks thoughts were disturbed by a knock on the workshop door.

"It's open," he said. "Come in or go away."

"Richard may we have a word?" Nicolas said.

The whole Bekenbaum tribe was behind him, including Rudy, who was looking around the workshop, his eyes stopping at all of the sports trophies Rick had gathering dust on shelves and medals Rick had received, both sports and military, hanging by their ribbons seemingly at random around the room. There were pictures of sports teams with championship trophies and pictures of men and women in combat uniforms all over the room.

"What can I do for you General?" Rick asked. Automatically he assumed the position of parade rest, his feet shoulder width apart with his hands bunched behind the small of his back and his eyes looking two inches above his grandfather's head.

"Richard this is personal," Nicolas said.

Rick let his eyes drop and saw that all of the adults were standing as Rick was, at parade rest. The room was silent, except for the sound of Rudy's feet as he slowly pivoted around the room looking at everything. The sound of Elizabeth clearing her throat brought Rudy back to the purpose that he had been brought here for.

"Uncle Richard, I would like to apologize for my behaviour at the game," Rudy said.

Rick looked down at his nephew and saw that he was going through the motions, like anyone at his age would do, when forced to do what he did not want to do. Rick took a deep breath and let it out slowly. He walked over, put his arm around his nephew's shoulders and guided him to look at a group of three pictures.

"These pictures were taken by your grandmother Rudy," Rick said. "The one on the left is of your father and me. Olds beat us good that day. I got to play the last five minutes of the game and had one sack, two hurries and a pass knocked down. Your father came over and congratulated me on my play. Me, the third string, fifteen year old first year player being congratulated by the all-star quarter back and captain of the team that trounced us 60 to 0."

Rick turned Rudy to the second picture. This one of a group of players in football uniforms, Didsbury on their uniforms, tossing helmets in the air, jumping and hugging each other and he went back to that time and began to talk. Olds had won every game that season and the games that Didsbury had played against them had all been blow outs. Two thirds of the Olds team were grade twelve students who had played the last three years together. The Didsbury team was much younger, smaller and weaker than the Olds team. Even so the Didsbury team had won enough games to make it to the playoffs and had won, barely, the first playoff game. This won them the dubious honour of facing the older, tougher, veteran Olds squad for the divisional championship.

By half time, Olds was up 28 to 0 and Didsbury could generate no offence and the defence had just suffered injuries to their starting middle linebacker and strong safety. That meant that Rick and Harold, the Geek Squad, would have to play. The mood in the Didsbury dressing room was gloomy as they all felt another blow out was in progress.

"Shit Rick," Harold had said. "You know they are going to be picking on both of us. We're up the creek without a paddle."

"Maybe so Harold," Rick had said. "But I'm not going to lay down and let them run over me. If I see you doing that, I'm gonna kick your butt."

Didsbury kicked off to start the second half and were able to stop Olds at their own 38 yard line. Rick lined up and knew they would run right up the centre right at him. He evaded the block from the on rushing fullback and put all of his 135 pounds into hitting the onrushing freight truck that was the half back, holding him up long enough for his defensive buddies to come and knock him down, holding Olds to a five yard gain. The next play, the halfback went between the left guard and tackle and Rick hit him just below the knees and wrapped both arms around the running backs legs tripping him up and holding him for a three yard gain, two yards short of a first down. Olds decided to play it safe and punt, not only for the first time that game, but the first time all year against Didsbury.

Their punter shanked the ball and Didsbury took position on their own 45 and managed to get a first down before having to punt and pinning Olds back on their 25. At the snap of the ball, Rick took a risk and charged the line, side stepping the astonished centre and full back and grabbing the half back just as he received the handoff from the quarterback and dropping him for a three yard loss. The next play Olds tried to take advantage of Rick, by a screen play, but Rick had read the play and was back in coverage, knocking the ball down and forcing another punt. Didsbury scored a field goal on the ensuing offensive plays. The first points they had scored against Olds all season. The mood of the team began to change.

"Game ain't over yet," Rick said in the defensive huddle. "We win one play at a time, one tackle at a time one broken block at a time. That's all that matters."

The next play, Olds tried to power sweep around the end, but what the Didsbury team lacked in size they made up for in speed and stopped Olds for only a two yard gain. Next they tested Harold who was up to the task and knocked down the pass, forcing another Olds punt. Olds held them to three and out, but the ensuing punt had Olds once again on their 25. Now they were staying away from Rick, going off tackle, but Rick was still there adding to the tackle and holding them to a two yard gain. They went down field again testing Harold who intercepted the ball and ran it back to the ten setting up a Didsbury touchdown. 28-10 halfway through the third quarter. Again Didsbury forced Olds to punt from their own thirty. This time the offence scored a touchdown and Olds was in trouble. 28-18 at the end of the third. Olds went back to what had been working for them in the first half and while they were able to generate a couple of first downs, the fired up Didsbury team held them on their own side of the field. The Didsbury offence once again drove down the field and scored another touchdown, 28-25, with two minutes left in the game. Now both teams were serious. Both teams determined to win. Olds drove out to their 45 and Didsbury stopped them, Rick sacking the quarter back for a five yard loss. Olds needed only a first down to win the game and they went for it, going deep at second and fifteen. Rick was able to hurry the quarterback and he made a bad pass that Harold easily picked off, running it back for a touchdown. Rick supplied the key block that let Harold run into the end zone untouched. 28-32. Olds had less than a minute to score at least a field goal to force overtime.

Nobody said a thing in the huddle. All the Didsbury players knew what was on the line. Olds went long on the first play taking the ball to Didsburys 50, but not getting out of bounds. They had one play, maybe two at most left. Knowing they had to go long, Didsburys defensive backs were lined up twenty yards back. The ball was put into play and Rick made sure they were not coming into his area then let out after the quarter back who was scrambling around trying to buy time for one of his receivers to break free. He didn't even see Rick streaking in from the blind side and dropping him ten yards behind the line of scrimmage. The gun sounded signalling the end of the game and the quiet stands erupted in cheers. Didsbury had done the impossible. They had beaten Olds.

Now Rick turned Rudy to the last picture. It was the same two players as the first one. This time the Olds player had the Didsbury player in a bear hug lifting him off the ground.

"The Olds player was your dad Rudy," Rick said. "The shrimpy Didsbury player was me. Your father was even more gracious in defeat than he was in victory. Respect must be earned Rudy, it cannot be demanded or ordered. Everyone in this room knows that but you Rudy.

The people that follow your mother, have and will follow her to the gates of hell if she takes them there. The same was with your father. I would have gone and done anything he asked of me and never questioned it."

The whole time, Rick had been speaking just above a whisper, but everyone in the room had heard every word he had spoken. The women were openly crying.

"Fate has given everyone in this room a large burden Rudy, not just you. Everyone looks to us for direction. Everyone expects us to come up with the right plan. There is no way we can be everything to everybody. We do not know everything, but everyone expects us to. We rely on others to give us the answers we seek and we make the decisions based on those answers. For that, we need their respect and respect can only be earned. It can only be earned by being willing to do whatever task, menial that it may be, that needs doing."

"But I only want them to like me," Rudy said. "How do I do that?"

"By doing the best that you can in everything you do. By being humble. By not lording your position over anyone. By being willing to sacrifice yourself to help another person out.

"Come with me, I'll show you how to start," Rick said, picking up a tennis ball from a shelf and heading outside.

Behind the workshop was a fence with a number of faded, crudely drawn squares drawn on it, high and low and centre.

"You're scared of the ball Rudy," Rick said. "A tennis ball is the same size and shape as the ball you use."

Rick began throwing the ball against the fence. At first lightly and slowly, then picking up speed and force and he was soon running side to side, making it harder and harder on himself to catch the rebounds, until finally, he failed.

"He did that for hours, every day," Emily said. "It used to drive us nuts, bang, bang, bang. All day long. We always knew when he was having a bad day. He went longer and harder."

"Don't push it Rudy," Rick said. "This exercise will help you learn how to react to the ball. It will also help you with your hand eye control and with your batting. Your coach now knows to treat you like any other kid and he will. The harder you practice, the better you will get and the more you will play. Just do your best. Sometimes it will be good enough, sometimes not. All that matters is that you try. Can you do that?"

"Yes sir," Rudy said.

"Good," Rick said tossing the ball to Rudy. "Use this until you can get your own."

"Come on Rudy," Emily said. "I want to show you my new colt and then maybe a cookie?"

"Oh yes please granma," Rudy said and the elder Bekenbaums shepherded the young man along.

"Thank you Rick," Elizabeth said, through the tears and she hugged Rick close. "I was overlooking everything just as you said. I was over compensating for his not having a father."

"Ya I know sis," Rick said. He held her head to his chest and stroked her hair gently. "I had pop and Oppa, but I still had to figure out stuff for myself, just like you did. Hopefully what was said here rubs off."

"You didn't see the way he was looking at you while you were telling your story," Elizabeth said. "He would look at those pictures and then back at you. He sees how small you were then and believe me he has heard the stories about you and Harold, 'The Geek Squad'. And his father. I think he feels he needs to be as good, or better than you. I think you may have made a buddy here."

"Ya, well," Rick said. "Now go find him before grandma fills him full of sugar and stuff."

After Elizabeth left, Rick resumed his research on the training camps in Afghanistan, once again losing touch with time. He was so engrossed, that he did not notice Emily come in and put a thick file on his desk and stand watching him for a while. It was not until she moved behind him, put her hands gently on his forearms and kiss him on the top of the head, that he became aware of her presence.

"That was good work you did with Rudy today Richard," she said softly. "There may be hope for you yet."

"He needed that a long time ago," Rick said. "We have all been codling him for to long now. We are going to need him in about ten years."

"Yes, and Liz is adamant about staying true to Rudy Sr. She refuses to look for another mate. Speaking of which, why are you here on your leave working? How am I ever going to get a daughter in law with you working all the time? You should be out clubbing with your buddies in Red Deer or Calgary."

"Well ma, for one thing, the poor girl has to compete with you, Omma and Liz. No small feat, I assure you. The bar is rather high. Next, they either find out I have a lot of money and very good connections, or I am in the Army and like being in it. Not only that, but I am not a commissioned officer. I don't want to have any part of the first group and the ones in the second group don't want any part of me."

"The right girl will come along Richard" Emily said. "It did for Nicolas and your father. I had no idea your father was anything more than a part time soldier and oil pipeline worker when I met your him. He thought I was just a freelance photo journalist. It all worked out. And as far as the poor girl measuring up. She doesn't have to compete with Tatiana like I did. Now there was a woman. She and Christine and Sandy and the original Elizabeth and most of the Bekenbaum women. But we manage somehow. Now what are you working on?"

Rick elaborated on how he thought that sometime in the near future, the Regiment would have to send a commando to Afghanistan to put down some of the terrorist training camps. He was working on which ones were the worst threats and possible ways of completing the missions.

"We in the Staff have not been sitting on our hands Gadget," Emily said. "Harold is being given his own platoon, as is Sandy. We need them to expand our capabilities using the drones. With you, that gives us three teams with those capabilities should we need them. That leaves your crew a little short. But what we really need from you right now, is what you have been training that new group for. In light of that, we have given you six people to make up a full commando complement. You will have command. Their files are on your desk. We have already come up with a plan and a group of locals that are willing to help us. When the time comes, you have to be fully ready to go, so you will need to start planning and training, at the latest by the beginning of August. All of those people in those files are top notch, but mechanized warriors. You will have to go back to basics with them."

Rick quickly glanced through the files and recognized every name. Each of them, without exception, had used the more rigorous trials to graduate with their Eagles. Just like he, Bill and Julia had.

"I think I have a problem," Rick said. "Pat does not have the equestrian skills as far as I know. She comes from Olds and they have a different tradition there."

"Sergeant Stewart comes from a long line of cavalry people Rick. She has extensive experience in ranching. She was also top notch in Empennage competitions and a superb barrel racer. I think she will be just fine," Emily replied.

"If you say so ma," Rick said, picking up his cell phone and speed dialling a number on it.

"Pat, it's Rick. Listen, are you doing anything pressing for the next four days? Well I am sure the Big Hunk will understand when I tell him. He and Julia will be joining us anyway. Ok, we will be living out of saddle bags, so just bring your bedroll and a few extra cloths. Bill will bring up pack horses with other stuff, so let Julia know what you need. All in all, we will be out there for about a month. Call it bonding time if you will. Ok, I want to get out of here by nine tomorrow. I supply the horses and the gear. See you then."

Then he dialled another number and told Bill to meet them at the Panther clearing on Monday with enough supplies to last a month, with a final call to Julia to coordinate with Bill and Pat.

"Colonel, please have the rest of the commando meet us at the Ranger Creek staging area the Tuesday after the August long weekend. We need supplies for a month for the whole commando. I want Russian weaponry and ammo and oh yes, our swords. Get a decent one for Pat. We'll come in after Labour Day."

"Will you need transport back here?" Emily asked writing all this down.

"No, we'll ride back. Leave the files here, I will look at them tonight. Please say goodbye to Liz and Rudy for me. I'm going to be a bit busy."

Chapter Two

Rick had his horse saddled before Patricia showed up and he observed how she went about adjusting equipment and saddling her horse. She was definitely not a novice. She quickly stowed her gear in the two saddle bags, hung her water jug around the horn and tied her sleeping bag with her slicker wrapped around it, to the back of the cantle. Like Rick, she was wearing cowboy boots, but with blunt toes and walking heels. Her pants were tucked into the boots and unlike Rick, she was wearing spurs. Both of them had felt cowboy hats on with chin straps and both had lined jean jackets with down vests on over long sleeved heavy cotton shirts.

In answer to Rick's question if she was ready, Pat swung into the saddle and then raised her eyebrows as Rick firmly put his knee into his horses belly and tightened his cinch. He ignored her unspoken question and taking the lead out of the home yard, broke into a trot down the trail. Ten minutes later, Pat asked for a stop and she got off, readjusted her saddle and tightened her cinch.

"Don't you have to do the same?" she asked.

"Well for one thing," Rick said. "I can ride without a saddle, having one is just more comfortable for me. For another, these horses aren't dumb. They take a big breath when you first pull on the cinch, so of course it comes loose after a bit and you have to readjust everything. A horse is like a teenager, they think they know what's best for them, but a loose saddle causes back sores. So a little punch in the belly so that they let out their breath when you tighten the cinch, is actually better for them. But, what do I know?

"The same with the trot right away. You'll see now that they will be settled right down and walk nicely without all the fuss you are used to."

This proved itself out moments later when they set out, this time at a brisk walk.

After being asked, Pat told Rick about her Purebred barrel racing and show horses. How they were bigger than Rick's horses.

"Can your horses trot all day?" Rick asked. "Can they do that day after day while living on only grass and being outdoors sometimes for months? These ones can. They will also kick the shit out of your big Purebreds. These are Cossack horses. They are not bred to be fast or beautiful. They are bred for stamina and intelligence. In fact I'm amazed Willy hasn't tried to throw you yet. But I am sure that will come."

"Are these part of the original bloodline?" Pat asked. "I've heard a lot about them."

"Well, Barney here, he is a direct descendant to old Bartholomew, Andreas's horse. There is always somebody in the family who keeps up the breeding program. Mom has taken that over ever since I got a little to busy doing other things. Nicolas has started back into it, as has pop."

They spent the rest of the day talking horses and ranching. Rick asked her about her show ring riding and barrel racing and her breeding programs.

"I want to show you something you may have heard about but never seen," Rick said. "You just stay there a little off the trail."

Rick rode down the trail about a hundred yards and dropped his hat on the ground then rode a further hundred yards, spun Barney around and went to a full gallop from a standstill. He took both feet from the stirrups and swung completely underneath the galloping horse, then flipped onto his back on top of the saddle, then looped his right knee over the saddle horn and dropped down until his head was almost touching the ground and picked his hat off the ground as he flashed by, finishing off by sitting backwards in the saddle, then flipping into a handstand and plunking back down in the saddle facing forward, jamming his hat on his head and stopping right in front of Pat.

"That is the difference between English riding and Cossack riding," Rick said. "That is also why Cossack Cavalry is better than English Cavalry. Julia can do almost as much of that as I can and Bill is not far behind."

"Bill?" Pat said. "Bill from the LA Hood can do those things?"

"Almost all of them, he is still learning. I'll make him demonstrate when he gets here. Come on, let's unsaddle these ponies and let them have some food and make our own. I don't know about you, but it's been a while since I was on horseback. We have some miles to make tomorrow, so early to bed for me I am afraid."

Rick kept the mood light for the next two days and they arrived early to the clearing on the Panther. Both of them took the time to ready the horse holding area and to clear the camp spot of fallen branches and gather sufficient fire wood for a couple of days. By the time they were finished, Bill and Julia arrived, dragging two pack horses each behind them. It was getting cool and the sun was beginning to go behind the mountains by the time everyone was finished unloading the pack horses and setting up the two small tents for sleeping. Bill had brought a six pack of beer and he brought it out and plunked it in the small stream to cool, while Rick cooked the last of the fresh chicken the new comers had brought on the small grill he had placed over the open fire.

"I can't get over the contrast," Julia said. "Two hours from here is Calgary, with its high rise offices, noise and hustle and bustle. Here, except for the odd high altitude contrails of passing airplanes, it's almost like we are all alone in the wilderness."

They had finished cleaning the small amount of dishes they had used and packed them away. Bill and Rick were in the process of hoisting the box holding the fresh meat ten feet off the ground on a tree limb and the two girls were laying on elbows next to the fire, relaxing.

"Ya, well Mr, Grizzly comes by for a snack tonight and you might wish more people were still around," Bill said.

"Oh, I am sure that 44 magnum you have tucked into the small of your back will discourage Mr. Grizzly well enough," Rick said. "Doesn't that hurt your back while you're riding?"

"Ya, some," Bill agreed. "But it is better than having some do gooder tree hugger, running to the Fish Cops and reporting me."

"Well my son," Rick said. "Mr. Remington here is a much better solution I think."

Rick walked over to his saddle and pulled a Remington 12 gauge pump shotgun out of the scabbard attached to the saddle.

"Two sold slug shot, followed by three antipersonnel 32 caliber buckshot and Mr. Griz is not a problem anymore. And seeing as we look like ranch hands, the do gooders expect to see rifle scabbards on our saddles. Another day and it won't matter until we get to the Ranger Creek drop off to pick up the others. Nobody but die hards goes this far back in the bush anyway."

"Others? What others?" Pat asked. "We have to be back at base for duty in two weeks."

"We will be linking up with the six new members of our commando there Pat," Rick said. "From there, we will start training in the techniques we will most likely be using on our next assignment. All nine of us are Cossack trained Pat, almost before we could walk. The other reason you and I spent a few days alone together, was for me to assess your mounted skills. If you choose to stay with us, the three of us will impart some of our training to you, so you are not completely in the dark."

"If I choose? What does that mean?" Pat said.

"Our next mission will be way behind the lines. The only support we will have is from the locals. These locals are rather primitive and are a warrior and horse based culture, not unlike our forefathers. You have some strikes against you right out of the gate. You are a foreigner, you ride funny, you are a woman and you are black. The gender and the colour will go away after they can see what you can do. The culture and the religion thing, well maybe not so much. We will be with these people for a long time Pat. You need to think long and hard about this."

"If I choose not to come?" Pat asked.

"You will be assigned to a different commando and someone else will take your spot with us," Rick said. "There will be absolutely no penalty or consequences if you don't come Pat. Regiment had not include you in our original planning scheme."

"You three are going?"

"I don't have a choice Pat," Rick said. "The two other dummies volunteered."

Bill walked over to the little stream and brought out the now cool beer and passed them around. Pat took hers but did not open it. She sat looking into the fire, saying nothing as the others quietly sipped their beer, not intruding on her brooding. After a few minutes of staring into the fire, Pat reached for one of her saddle bags and brought out a bottle of schnapps. She spun the top off the bottle and tossed it into the fire, looked up to the heavens and screamed a long undulating scream.

"Fuck it, I'm in!" She yelled, taking a deep pull on the bottle before passing it around. "Where you idiots go, so do I."

Bill let out a deep roar after taking a big gulp of the fiery liquid and grabbed Patricia up off the ground and swung her around, before pulling her close and kissing her hard. When he let her go, she grabbed his head, pulled it down to her and kissed him hard right back.

"Don't even think about it Bill," Julia said after Bill had put Pat down and was looking at her. "Al will have your balls if you kiss me like that."

"And Miss Prissy will have mine if you kiss me, you lunk," Rick said.

Rick and Julia were trying hard not to laugh, but the look on the two lovers faces made it impossible. Soon they were both laughing hard.

"What's so damn funny?" Patricia said, stomping her foot.

"Oh Mr. Jackson?" Rick said in a falsetto voice. "May I have a moment of your time? I have something you should look at."

"But of course Sergeant Stewart," Julia said, mimicking Bills deep voice. "Anything you need."

"Why thank you Mr. Jackson. You are always so thoughtful."

"Always here to help the troopers Sergeant Stewart."

"Oh shut up!" Patricia said, throwing a piece of firewood at Rick and Julia. Bill was just looking at his shoes.

"Why Rick," Rick said, deepening his voice. "Did you see how she looked at me at lunch? Do you think I should ask her out?"

"Jules," Julia said. "Bill and Rick are buddies aren't they? Can you ask Rick what Bill thinks of me? Am I pretty enough do you think? All the other girls are always looking at him."

"Ah shit," Bill said. "And here we thought nobody knew."

"Well if you don't mind," Rick said, picking up his sleeping bag and tarp. "I'm going to go sleep by the horses. It's bound to be quieter than around here tonight."

"Well I'm going down by the creek," Julia said. "That's all I need. Listening to two dogs in heat and me three days from my Al."

"Right," Rick said walking back to the camp fire the next morning after breakfast with a four foot long canvas bag in his hands. He undid the bag and pulled out four, three foot long swords encased in their scabbards.

"This is a standard issue Cossack sword," he said, tossing one to Patricia, then handing the other two their personal weapons.

"We carry them across our backs, hilts above the left shoulder, even when dismounted," he said, draping his across his back and adjusted the straps so that it was firmly attached. "Julia help her adjust it will you?"

The four of them walked over to the horses and saddled up.

"Demonstration time," Rick said. "I showed you some fancy riding the other day. Those moves have a purpose and a function. Bill slow motion if you please."

Bill pulled out his sword and advanced on Rick at a walk with the point aimed at Ricks heart. Two steps from Bill, Rick pulled his sword and kicking his feet from the stirrups, laid back on the horses back. Bills sword went over Rick, who pivoted up and to the left, bringing his sword across the back of Bills neck. As the two walked away from each other, Rick flipped all the way around so he was facing backwards and mimicked shooting Bill in the back with a rifle. Then flipping back forward, still at the walk, he advanced on the two women and dropped to the off side of the horse so that his body was shielded by the horse and reaching under the animal's neck, again made the motions of firing a rifle at the two women. Again flipping up and facing to the rear of the animal, firing at them again as he rode away. Coming back, he swung down off the side of the animal and picked up a now kneeling Julia, swinging her up behind him on the saddle. Bill riding back to the group, also swung down off the side of his horse and deftly picked up Rick's fallen sword from the ground.

"Do you see now?" Rick asked. "You may need those skills in addition to the basic cavalry drill you were given in Olds. We also shoot off our horses, as well as deploying in a skirmish line on foot. You will need to master that. You and Julia will be our horse holders in action. You need to be able to hit a target while at the gallop. You also need to lose those spurs. You hit that horse with them and you will find yourself on your ass, in the dirt.

"Oh, and here is what your Dressage movements are really supposed to look like and what their real purpose is."

Rick lead his horse through several complicated movements, each time the horse threw out a hoof in a violent kick, or side step. Sometimes accompanied with a vicious simulated bite. The finale, was rearing up and punching fore hooves at head height. Then rearing back with both hind feet, kicking hard and rotating around in a circle unguided, doing the same movements while Rick slashed his sword left and right.

"These horses, while generally good people, like us, when motivated are deadly killers." Rick said.

"Now you have two weeks to become somewhat competent in these techniques. You won't be a complete embarrassment to us when we meet the rest of the gang."

The normal daily routine consisted of two members of the group fixing breakfast while the other two watered and fed the horses at day break. They would break camp and ride for four hours, until finding a suitable spot. Then, would have a quick lunch and proceed another four hours finding a good camping spot and setting up for the evening. They would do a half hour of training before rubbing down their mounts and having dinner. At the beginning of the second week, Rick handed each member of the little group a set of operating manuals.

"This is for the AK74M rifle. We will be using those in country," Rick said. "They have similar ballistics to what we are used to. The bullet is roughly the same and ammo is plentiful where we are going. Bill and I will have grenade launchers, just as we have now. There will be two RPKMs just as we have two minimis, they utilize the same cartridge as the AK74s but have a larger magazine. You will need to be familiar with those as well. In addition, we will have two snipers. One light sniper using an SVDU semi automatic, firing a 7.62 round and the other, a KVSK, utilizing a 12.1 cartridge. Again similar to what we are using with our NATO equipment.

"We will receive the weapons after we link up with the rest of the commando and start field training with them at that time. Julia and Pat, you will be our comms people as well as assault troops. We will be using our own comms, so transition will be no problem for you."

"Can you tell us the target yet?" Bill asked.

"Not really," Rick said. "It will be in a remote part of Afghanistan, that's all the info I have right now."

For the most part, the four friends had the back country trails to themselves and the wildlife. More often than not, they were able to supplement their rations with fresh rainbow or brown trout taken from the glacier fed streams. The trip was more like a holiday than a working trip and the four became closer and tighter as a group. Julia had days when she missed Al dearly and Rick became her shoulder to cry on and confidant. On more than one occasion, she expressed her gratitude for the Bekenbaum family taking her and her family in and one night around the camp fire Patricia asked why. Julia was still to embarrassed to talk about her family, so Bill explained in her stead.

Julia's mother and father had worked hard to provide for their families. The father had risen to be foreman of his crew at the factory and the mother had worked as a home care provider at the local retirement lodge. Then the factory owner's decided to shut the plant down and move it to China to increase their profits, which basically destroyed the small town's economy over night. Unable to make their mortgage commitments, the family had lost everything and moved to a low cost rental in a trailer park. Unlike Canada, the lower rent districts in America were riven with crime and substance abuse issues. Schools were subpar compared to the more affluent areas and opportunities were few and far between to better themselves.

"As bad as we had it in the Hood," Bill said. "At least we could blame discrimination or the Whitey's for holding us down. Julia's family and those like her had no excuse. A White person is expected to work hard and do well in America. There are few assistance programs for whites. Pat, these folks here, they don't notice your colour. Back home, there is no way you would have gotten the same opportunities you have here. Even when you're rich, being black in America is hard."

"Yes that's why I quit going down there to Barrel race," Patricia said. "It was just to much trouble to be worth it. I went to Virginia to compete with the Canadian equestrian team and was treated like a leaper by most of the American competitors."

"Yes, well that is America and not here," Rick said. "We have our problems here to, but they are nowhere near as bad. Pats great whatever granddaddy, was a Buffalo Soldier and had a college education. The army would only allow him to be a sergeant, not an officer. He fought with distinction in Cuba, yet received no awards for it. He was coming up here anyway when he ran into our bunch. Andreas quickly took him in and we have been reaping the rewards ever since. I think it is just dumb to discriminate because of skin colour or nationality or religion or whatever. The Germans might have won the second world war if they had not wasted all the man power and material used for the final solution with the Jews. Not only that, but they wasted the very potential of those same people to help with the war effort. You see the same thing all over the world. Zimbabwe was feeding all of Africa until they kicked the white people out and had the second best economy in Africa. Now they are starving to death. Muslim killing Muslim, Christian killing Christian. Blacks killing blacks. It's all stupid."

"That's an interesting point of view based on your current occupation Rick," Patricia said.

"Yes I am a soldier and I am good at it," Rick said after a moment. "That doesn't mean I like it. I would like nothing better than to go play with my horses and work on the pipelines. Unfortunately, there are bad nasty people out there and if I and people like me don't stand up to them, we will end up like Zimbabwe or any number of Arabic countries run by a small group of vicious killers only intent on keeping their power and money. I do this so that normal people don't have to worry, can keep safe and sleep at night."

With that Rick stood up, gathered his sleeping bag and walked away from the fire pit. It wasn't often that he had an attack of conscience and doubted himself. He had done his bit, put in his five years. Now he could sit back, turn it all over to someone else and enjoy the rest of his life. He didn't need to prove anything to anybody anymore. He had enough money already, with more coming in from his designs, he need never to have to work again. While this outing was fun and the next few weeks would be more of the same, he knew it wouldn't last. They would be hot and dry in the day time and cold at night soon. They would be dirty and tired and hungry, relying on people they did not know, who could turn on them at any second. Far from home and any hope of support, they would be on their own and far from the comfort of family and friends. While the romantic novels relished in the glory of combat, they never told of the misery and deep, deep fear each man felt just before going into action. The sights, sounds and smells of battle, wounded crying and screaming in pain, the loss of a dear friend. The feeling of hopelessness as that friend lay dying and knowing there was nothing he could do about it.

And behind it all, knowing he would once again shoulder the burdens, the loneliness and the fear. Because in the end, he was a soldier and that's what soldiers do.

It was three days after Labor Day and the commando was finally far enough back in the bush, that they could set up targets and fire live ammunition without being bothered by well-meaning civilians. A notice had been sent to any of the guide and outfitters that may have thought of taking a party back in the area, to stay away, as there was a military training exercise underway. So the serious back country travellers would stay away and the commando were far enough back, that most recreational travellers would not be around. Hunting season would not start for another week, which would also eliminate further die hards from coming this far back.

"Well we have all had the last day to get a feel for the new weapons hanging across our backs," Rick said. "Me, I appreciate the folding stock. Snipers, how do you feel about carrying the carbine and extra rounds along with the rifles?"

"We don't think it's worth the extra fire power Gadget," Master Corporal Litzenberger said. "We both have forty rounds that we can do a lot of damage with. If it gets to the point where we need these carbines, it's probably going to be to late anyway."

"Ya, that's what I thought too," Rick said. "They might be ok for close quarters or indoors, but the short stock and barrels won't do much for accuracy along with the extra weight. Speaking of which, I don't plan on taking any armour or a helmet with me. These new rounds will punch right through anything we have right now and I want the mobility and less weight to cart around. I'll leave it up to each of you individually what you want to do, but I'd rather use the extra weight to carry a few more grenades for my launcher.

"Now I've been told that these weapons are comparable to what we are used to using. So let's get at it and find out, eh?"

They had exhausted all of the ammunition they had been issued for training and all of them had learned the weaknesses and strengths of the new weapons. They had fired them in the dark of night and it had snowed heavily one day as it is want to do in September in the Alberta High Country, then become hot the next day. They had practiced assaults and deploying from line of travel on horseback, to repelling an ambush on foot. By the time they reached the barracks at the end of the ten days, Rick felt they were as ready as they ever would be.

They gathered together for a last meeting in the mess club, in a room set aside for them. They had all showered and put on the blue jeans and t-shirts they wore as civilians.

"Ok, I kind of know what our targets will be," Rick said. "But at this time I can't say for sure. Nor can I say, when or if, we will be deployed. These training camps have become a sore point and the graduates are causing a lot of grief around the world, so I think we will be sent in, just not the time frame. So let's all go home and be with our families. Be back here next Monday and we'll do some more work with the weapons, but it will be daytime work only, you'll go home everyday."

Rick was the first one to leave and he was soon fast asleep in his single bed at the back of his workshop.

Chapter Three

All to soon, his cell phone was ringing and he ignored it. Then it rang again and again and as he had decided he should probably answer it the next time it rang, someone was pounding on the workshop door.

"What the fuck!" he said, pulling the door open, to see a fully armed trooper standing at the door.

"The General wants you in the briefing room ASAP! Two airplanes have flown deliberately into the World Trade Centre in New York."

Rick hurriedly pulled on his jeans and a shirt, jammed his feet into his boots and jogged behind the trooper to the headquarters building, which was a beehive of activity and more people were arriving by the minute, some in uniform, but most without. He was ushered into the large briefing room and a six foot screen was at the front, showing the CNN coverage of the event. The room was full and hushed, the shot of the two buildings burning taking up the whole screen. Then in a cloud of dust and smoke, one building collapsed.

"Warrant Bekenbaum," Nicolas said, spying Rick at the back of the silent room. "Your Commando has been activated and the members notified and on their way. We are arranging air transport for you now. Warrant Jackson will be here momentarily and you are to meet with the intel people when he gets here."

Before anything else could be said, CNN cut to another reporter who said the Pentagon had also been hit and there were reports that another airliner had been high jacked and was suspected of being on its way to the capital. The president and cabinet had been sent away and that all airspace in the United States had been shut down.

"Shit," was all that Nicolas said. "We are at war folks."

Rick and Bill were standing at the front of the small briefing room as the rest of the commando filed in. Both men were wearing desert camouflage uniforms, on their feet wore the modern version of the cavalry boots made famous by the RCMP. Their modified Stetson hats were laying on the table behind them. Both men surveyed the commando as they filed in, wearing their civilian clothing.

"A terrorist organization has hit the United States of America," Rick started. "At this time, at least two buildings of the World Trade Centre in New York have collapsed, trapping hundreds of people inside. Another plane has hit the Pentagon and still another has crashed short of its suspected target, the white house. This is an act of war against a NATO member and we have been activated. This Regiment, by way of our special status is now at war with the organization or organizations behind this act.

"Suitable air transport has been arranged and we will be leaving as soon as you can get geared up. We will be changing aircraft in Frankfurt, from where we will be dropped directly at our first target. Full battle loads people and no, I repeat no markings, other than your identity disks and the Canada flash are permitted on this mission. You are not permitted any communications from now on. Your families will be notified of your deployment by the Regiment. Further briefing will be held once we leave Frankfurt. Dismissed."

"Don't we need authorization from DND and parliament to deploy?" Bill asked once the commando had left the room.

"The Queen has ordered the Earl to make ready and to deploy whatever resources we have available," Rick said handing Bill a sheet of paper.

"Oh ya," Bill said reading it. "I keep forgetting that."

'We order Our Earl, the Lord Richard Bekenbaum, to make ready to defend Our Realm and to go to the aide of Our ally the United States of America and render what immediate and future assistance that he can."

The private jet, escorted by a series of pairs of fighter jets landed in Frankfurt Germany nine hours later and they were sent to a hanger away from prying eyes and not allowed to leave the aircraft until it was inside the hanger with the hanger doors closed.

"OK, you've got an hour to do whatever you have to do then we board that beasty," Rick said, pointing at a Hercules transport plane with German national markings on it. "We have another eight hour trip and the end of it won't be as pleasant as this one is. The parachutes and our gear will be loaded on it for us and we can gear up on route. From this point forward, we talk Russian. Once we get on the ground, we talk German among ourselves unless we are addressing our friends on the ground over there."

Rick walked over to where a gaggle of German officers were gathered and introduced himself as Warrant Smith and asked for any updates and weather information at the target sight.

"Jean Akerman, CIA," a man in civilian clothing said, sticking his hand out to Rick. "You the same Warrants Smith and Wesson that handled that business with the Natives a while back?"

"I don't think so," Rick said. "What native business? I think you will find the names Smith and Wesson are very prevalent in the Canadian Forces."

"Ya, I keep forgetting you JTF2 people are super secret types," Akerman said. "No matter, you are here. You will be given sat sets and I will relay your orders through them. Here is a time schedule for your comms. You will be the first on the ground. We have some SF people on the way, but they are still in the planning stages and will be a while before they can take command of the situation. Until then you receive orders from me. We are working on getting you some support from the locals, but at this time nothing has been firmed up yet. I don't know what the rush is, you have no target yet."

"I have been instructed to hit my first target no later than 24 hours from now, which won't be a problem," Rick said. "Our Allies should be linking up with us at that site shortly after to conduct us to our second target. Hopefully you will have air assets in theatre by that time to help us out, but it won't be fully necessary to accomplish the mission.

"Like your country, mine operates on a need to know basis and obviously you do not need to know or you would have this information already. You and your people in theatre are free to ask us to perform missions for you, but the final decision to act or not is mine, not yours."

"You people have assets in country? How can that be, we barely have any and none in the region you are talking about. And how the hell did you pull all of this together so fast. We are still working on getting NATO approval."

"We have had assets in country for better than a hundred years," Rick said. "It's not our problem you people keep disregarding the intel we send you. The only surprise about this attack, was the number and the targets themselves. We have been planning this for almost a year now. As far as getting approval. A good friend doesn't wait to be asked when a friend is in trouble. A good friend just acts. Now if you will excuse me, I have to coordinate with our German friends here."

"General Von Bekenbaum, so good to see you again," Rick said to his father's cousin in German.

"For me as well, Warrant Smith," the General said, shaking Rick's hand. "The assets your regiment has asked for are in place and we have a clear corridor directly to the drop zone. Your regiment has given us their latest intel on numbers of enemy in place, but I am afraid they will be many hours out of date by the time you arrive."

"Better than nothing," Rick said. "The Americans really dropped the ball this time eh?"

"They have to many agencies looking at to much data," The General said. "They tend to miss the forest for the trees. Does your government know you are here?"

"The head of state knows," Rick said. "The mood of the present government is such that they would like to get rid of the Army all together. Make us road and school builders. No doubt the Chief of Staff is conferring with the Americans right now and I have no doubt that JTF2 will be deploying soon. A rushed contingent of the PPCLI will be sent over and have to scrounge for fuel and ammunition like normal. The government will try to limit our involvement to as little as possible."

"I fear my governments response will be much the same," The General said. "There is still some reluctance to conduct offensive operations as fallout from the last war. But we will be there in some fashion. You let me know if you need anything. Oh and some of our Special Forces people are chomping at the bit to work with you. You take care cousin."

The commando walked up the rear ramp into the aircraft and were ushered to some jump seats along the walls toward the cockpit. Their canisters of gear and the parachute equipment was on a pallet that they walked around at the rear of the craft. As they made themselves comfortable, the hanger doors began to open and the large rear ramp of the aircraft began to close. A tug that had been waiting outside the hanger, hooked up to the front of the airplane and pulled it outside. Once disconnected, the pilot started the engines one by one and they were soon airborne.

Once they were in the air and the loadmaster had given him the ok, Rick gathered his people around and explained the situation to them. The training facility they would be assaulting had approximately a hundred people in it. They were mostly North American or European Muslim radicals that had joined in a misguided sense of duty to Islam. They would be trained to do any number of terrorist activities, from placing bombs at sporting events to shooting up shopping malls or suicide bombings. The facility was about ten kilometres from where the commando would be dropped and they would be dropped with about two hours of daylight left.

"In the Koran," Rick said. "It speaks of taking advantage of an enemy's Holy Days and religious habits when planning an attack. We will hit them at their morning prayers, just as the Koran suggests. We have another eight hour flight, so get some rest. Once we hit the ground there will be no time."

Rick left his people, walked up to the load master and asked him to wake him up two hours before the drop. Then he found a somewhat comfortable spot, laid down and went to sleep.

"It seems like we always end up back in Afghanistan," Nicolas said at the family meal. "We always seem to be drawn back there. What is the latest word?"

"The commando just left German airspace and should be on the ground in about eight hours," Paul said. "Our local friends are on their way but won't get there in time to help for the first assault."

"We have plans for a full battalion involvement in place?" Nicolas asked.

"Yes," Paul said. "But this Prime Minister, a, does not like us and b, will buck any kind of involvement at all. I don't think we need worry about deploying anytime soon. I do think though, that some of our other commando will be asked for. Either by the Americans or the British."

"I concur," Nicolas said. "Now to personal business Paul. Your mother and I have decided it is time to retire. We have met with the council, who are meeting with their people and I think you will be voted as the new Ataman. You will no longer be able to hide as a Master Warrant Officer and are promoted to General. Nor will you be involved in active military operations other than planning and overseeing them.

"I am eighty one years old and should have turned all this over to you years ago. You have good people on the staff that know their jobs and I would ask that you let them do it. Your mother and I will be leaving to visit your brother in Billings. With your over sight, he will take over control of our American owned assets. After that, we will be going to Europe to meet with the family there. With the demise of the Soviet Union, it is possible for us to visit the old family lands in Ukraine and we plan on doing that, as well as meeting with our lawyers in The Hague on a family matter that we are bringing forward to the World Court.

"Following that, we have arranged for some time with the Royal Family and then we will come home."

"Sounds more like work than a holiday," Paul said.

"Call it a working holiday," Nicolas said smiling. "One more thing. The current American President, I have no doubt in my mind, will take the current situation to finish what his father should have in Iraq. It will be your choice of course, but I would highly recommend that the regiment not become involved in that. It is a no win situation."

"Yes we have already been receiving discrete inquiries from the Americans and I agree, we should not become involved," Paul said. "The bigger long term threat is in Afghanistan and we should honour our agreements with our friends, both in America and in Afghanistan. No matter what the Americans say or how they spin it, Iraq was not behind the attacks. But the forces in Afghanistan were. As were some Saudis, who the Saudi Royal family are looking the other way on. The Americans are bound to retaliate by cutting us out of any of our business dealings in Iraq, but it won't stand up in court."

The next topic was Russia. With its new found mineral wealth, Russia was once again flexing its muscles and stirring up trouble in Europe. Funding and supporting breakaway regions of republics that had broken away, suppressing violently those who wanted to do the same with Russia. The new president had found a way to circumvent the

Russian constitution and still stay in power. They were trying to muscle Europe, this time by withholding supplies and demanding more money for Natural Gas supplies. So far they had Europe in a corner as the Europeans were importing thirty percent of their Gas from Russia, but they were actively working on a solution for that.

"That's one of the things I want to talk about in Germany," Nicolas said. "Building some liquid natural gas shipping ships. We still have an overabundance of gas here and lots of capacity in the pipeline going east. The Irving's have agreed to a partnership with us. We will build the facility and they will run it."

The family and the host had a ten percent share in the large original family company in Germany. They produced steel and ships. The LNG ship design that the company would produce would bring a further twenty percent in royalty revenue to the host, as would the LNG rail car design. The host and the family were already producing those cars in North America and leasing them to the shipping companies and railroads for a handsome profit. An LNG unloading facility was being negotiated with the German and other European governments, that both the Canadian and German branches of the family would own and operate.

Anticipating the rise in demand for Alberta crude oil that would result in an oil embargo because of the anticipated American invasion of Iraq, the demand for crude oil rail tanker cars was increasing, as was pipeline capacity to ship to the United States. The family had anticipated this demand and by a series of upgrades and new government approvals, had begun to lay new pipelines to American refineries. Pipelines had already been laid from the massive oil sands projects in northern Alberta, which were beginning to produce more oil each year as new technologies were unearthed to make extraction of the oil easier and more efficient.

Speculating that the seam of oil sands actually ran east west, the family had drilled a series of test holes and had obtained mineral rights in North Western Saskatchewan and North East British Colombia to extract the oil rich Bitumen, that they would sit on until the need arose. Already the projected reserves of oil in the north eastern Alberta oil sands projects was third only to Venezuela and Saudi Arabia. Once the true potential of the seam was realized, it would make Canada the largest oil producing country in the world. Once again the family was in the right place at the right time.

Royalties from the drone aircraft designs were pouring in, as both civilian and military uses for the aircraft were being realized. Contrary to most of the rest of the world, the company's other holdings in both the United States and Canada were doing well and making profits. Unlike other large North American Companies, the family had not shipped jobs to lower labor cost countries and had opted for lower profit for better quality and kept production in North America. At the same time, reaping profits from the companies that did ship from lower cost labor countries, by leasing containers, container rail cars and the German companies container ships.

As a result, the host had just finished upgrading all of their military equipment. Even the lowest and least used reserve units had more modern equipment than a lot of Canadian and Canadian allies front line troops had.

This brought the conversation back to Afghanistan and the projections of what the host would be asked to participate in. Transportation of equipment and material would be the biggest concern and the host had already obtained lease agreements with Ukraine for two heavy lift aircraft and had purchased two from Boing to operate itself. A search was on the way to find helicopters capable of operating in the altitudes that operations would have to be conducted in Afghanistan and several promising designs had been found and negations were underway to obtain them.

Paint and uniform camouflage schemes had been changed to reflect the conditions of that country and companies were being rotated to areas of the United States that had similar terrain for training. The regiment would be ready to go when asked to.

"Speaking of which, Rick should be ready to be inserted by now," Paul said. "He figures they will be twelve hours away from hitting that camp. I want to be in the comms room when that happens."

Chapter Four

Rick was awake at the first tap on his foot from the load master, who told him they were an hour and a half from the drop point. Rick nodded and looked around the interior of the airplane getting his bearings and noticing that most of his people were asleep. He yawned and then booted Bill twice on his foot and circled his finger to indicate it was time to wake up. Unbuckling his seat belt, Rick rose, stretching the kinks out before he walked to the cockpit. The flight engineer updated him on the latest weather and promised another just before the drop. He would be able to tell a lot from his Doppler radar, located in the nose, but conditions looked good.

Returning to the rear of the aircraft, Rick saw all his troopers going through their parachutes, making sure all was clear, secure and ready. Next was the sixty pound personal packs each trooper would carry. No loose flaps or gear could be allowed. The ten foot long strap that was attached to each pack and clipped to their harnesses, was attached firmly and would drop cleanly when the parachutes opened.

Rifles were examined one last time. Barrels and breaches clear, actions functioning properly and finally a loaded clip inserted. Those that smoked, lit a final cigarette. There would be no smoking once they exited the aircraft, the smell would give away their position, while the rest placed the packs between their feet and landed back against the walls of the plane. This was something they were all familiar and comfortable with. All of them had made over a hundred jumps, but each trooper handled the situation differently. Some were quiet and withdrawn, others gabby and loud. Rick went quickly through his preparations, as he was behind the rest time wise. Unlike the others, he motioned for another trooper to help him done his parachute. Adjusted the straps properly and then helped the trooper done his. This was the cue for everyone else to do the same.

While the commando had been making their preparations, the aircraft had slowly descended from 35000 feet to 10000 and a red light illuminated at the rear of the cargo bay. Even before the load master signalled them to rise and get ready, the commando were getting to their feet and hooking their static lines, five to a side, to a steel line that ran overhead down the length of the aircraft to the rear cargo door. When they were all hooked up, the lead trooper of each group of five standing at a spot five feet from the end of the aircraft and bracing themselves, the load master spoke into his head set and the pilot nosed over into a steep decent, while the load master decompressed the aircraft and listening for the signal, opened the large rear door once the plane had descended below 3000 feet, letting in the noise of the rushing air and the cold from the altitude. Once the plane levelled out, the commando moved to the edge of the door, closely bunched and when the overhead light changed from red to green, as a group, they ran out into the aircrafts slipstream. The aircraft was empty within ten seconds, the load master closed the door as the pilot gunned the plane to full speed and began to climb, rapidly banking the aircraft to return the way it had come.

They had been dropped at one thousand feet and the parachutes should open at about eight hundred. Each trooper hunched up waiting for the shock of the opening and then looking up to see if it was deployed properly, while dropping the packs they had held, to dangle below them. Once he had verified his chute was functioning properly, Rick glanced around quickly to gain his bearings and did a slow circle in his directional chute, locating the target about ten miles away. Then he checked over his commando and saw that all of the chutes had opened and that so far there were no concerns. Now he concentrated on the terrain he would fall into, made sure he was clear of any other trooper, looked out to the horizon, and bent his knees slightly waiting for his pack to hit the ground and flared the parachute, hard, once it did, coming to a standing stop once it did.

He hit his quick release on the parachute and expertly gathered it up, wrapping the cords around it to bundle it together. Unhooking his pack, he released his rifle and chambered a round, going to one knee and scanning his immediate area for danger. Then released his pack from its strap and quickly examining it for damage. Other troopers were doing the same and coming together to centre on Rick, dropping in a rough circle facing outwards and scanning the area for threats. Rick pulled his GPS unit from his cargo pocket on his pants and turned it on. While he was waiting for it to obtain his position, he pulled out his map from the same pocket. Once the GPS locked onto his position, he verified on the map where they were and turned it off again. As planned, they were ten miles from the target. While four troopers, one for each point on the compass, kept watch, the rest gathered up the bunched parachutes, dug a fast hole, dumped them in and covered them up. While this was going on, Bill came up to Rick.

"Everyone on the ground and safe," he said in Russian.

"Good, report it in," Rick said in the same language. "I want to be looking at that camp two hours before night fall, so we have to hustle."

In short order, the commando sorted themselves out and with the point element of three troopers ten yards in advance, they set out at a brisk pace in one meter intervals, one behind the other. Each trooper scanning the area, alternating from left to right down the single file they adopted. Two hours later, they were at the base of a small hill and while some made camp, Rick, Bill and one of the snipers crawled up to the edge, leaving only their heads exposed as they scanned the camp below with their binoculars.

There were ten, ten man tents arranged in rows. In the centre of the camp, were three large tents. One had to be the communications, tent as it had aerials poking out of it. One was the communal mess tent, which was confirmed as people began to emerge from it and in groups went to the sleeping tents. all but six. Three were dressed differently, in blue jeans and sweaters, while the other three were in green camouflage uniforms. The rest of the group were dressed head to foot in black.

"Shit," the sniper said. "Helicopter parked on the back side."

Rick moved his glasses to that area and confirmed that a small Bell helicopter in camouflage paint was parked to the rear of the camp. There were Pakistani identification markings on it and he pulled out the digital camera he had and focused the zoom lens on it, taking several photos and making sure he had the id numbers of the aircraft in several of them. Then he scanned back to the separate group and took photos of each of the six and as a group. While this was going on, the other hundred inhabitants of the camp came out to a flat area, spread their prayer carpets on the ground in lines of twenty five and began their evening prayers. Rick took a number of photos and then turned his attention to the camp itself.

The camp was in a small depression which would lend itself well to their planned assault and Rick picked out where he wanted to place his troopers. With a final look around, they crawled back down to the rest of the commando. Rick sent the rest up in groups of two to make their own observations and set up the radio and his small note book computer to make a quick burst transmission back to base once the communications satellite was in range.

"OK, no fires," Rick told the commando. "We need to keep covered until that helicopter leaves and we can't risk an assault until it leaves either. So we will just keep watch and look for patterns. I think the best plan is to hit them at morning prayers, but am open to suggestions."

The rest of the day was spent setting up camp and observing the target. Next morning Rick and Bill along with the large caliber sniper Al, were once again on the ridge line glassing the camp and as predicted, the enemy gathered for morning prayers in four lines of twenty five.

After prayers, they gathered in the large tent that served as the mess tent and had breakfast and before breakfast was over, the two Pakistani pilots walked over to the helicopter and began preparations to leave. Shortly after that, the last Pakistani approached with the three westerners and after shaking hands, the helicopter started up and the Pakistanis left in a cloud of dust and noise whirled up from the helicopters rotor blades. The camp settled down to a training day, which saw the group divide into two groups of fifty and go through whatever drills were on tap for the day.

The three Canadians slithered back down the hill and were replaced by two others, the plan being to keep the camp under constant observation. Pat gave Rick his note book computer and told him they had received a message from home base. The pictures they had taken the day earlier had been analysed. The three Pakistanis had been identified as members of Pakistan's equivalent to the CIA, one a high ranking officer. The three westerners were ex IRA radicals all with heavy bounties on their heads from the British government. Only one of the trainees had been identified so far and he was a Saudi radical whom the Americans had put a hefty bounty on.

"I hope we get a share of those bounties," Bill said. "I could use a new tractor."

"Only you would think of something like that," Julia said.

"What, I'm supposed to turn down good money?" Bill said.

"OK cut it," Rick said. "I think we should finish the job and get out of here safe before we start counting cash we don't have, or may never have."

After the sun went down and the enemy camp settled down for the night, the commando gathered together in a small circle in their fireless camp, shared out the MRE rations and after a few minutes of random chat, began to plan the next morning's assault.

Bill with his grenade launcher equipped AK74m, George with his RPKm, John and his light sniper rifle with Julia and her AK74m would take the front of the prayer group. Pat, Bob with the other RPKm, Sergei the medic and Calvin, would take the right side of the prayer group. Rick and Al, the large caliber sniper, would take the rear of the camp. The assault would start when Rick fired his grenade at the communications tent, followed by Bill doing the same. Bill would have the dual task of watching the left side for anyone trying to escape on that side. The attack would be sudden, violent and hopefully brief. No survivors were anticipated.

After a few more minutes of tidying up the small details, the talk shifted to more mundane matters about home and personal kidding around and after a while, the commando slowly drifted to their sleeping bags, leaving only Rick and Calvin who would be taking the first shift of watch and they moved to their positions keeping lookout for any passersby who might discover their existence. Although Rick was aware of his surroundings, his mind wandered, going over all the possible scenarios of what could happen the next day. They were out there all alone and far from help and while they were well trained, the possibility of getting killed or injured was always there. To soon, he was relieved and spent the rest of the night, mind racing on what he needed to do and how to do it.

"I don't know how he does that," Bill said pointing over at Rick while they all rose to get ready.

"Ya, it's always the same," Julia said. "There he is sleeping away sound as a baby. I didn't sleep a wink last night."

"That's one cool customer for sure," Al agreed. "Come on Sleeping Beauty, it's time to go."

Al and Rick had the furthest to go and set out first in the predawn dark and stillness. There was enough light from the moon and the stars up in the clear air of the high altitude, that they could see well enough not to trip and stumble on obstacles. It still took a long time to get into their location, about 100 meters from the rear of the target and take up their positions. As usual, the enemy had posted no sentries and there was nothing to alert them of the impending commando raid. Even though Rick knew where the positions of his troopers were, he could not detect them while he scanned their areas with his binoculars. Soon, the enemy was coming out of their tents to make their morning preparations, then began to gather with their prayer mats for morning prayers.

Rolling on his side, Rick ejected his thirty round clip, made sure the bullets were aligned right and reinserted it, pulling back the slide to charge the weapon. Then he flipped the lens caps off his two power scope and quickly sighted through it, making sure it was ok. Reaching into his right cargo pocket, he removed a fragmentation grenade for his grenade launcher and inserted it in the launcher under the barrel of his rifle. He looked over at Al, who having finished his preparations nodded at him.

Rick rose to one knee, wrapped his sling around his left arm, then sighted the weapon so that the grenade would exploded above the communications tent, pulled the trigger and seconds later, Armageddon rained down on the unsuspecting terrorists. The range was long for the grenade launcher, the grenade burst two meters short but a meter high and rained the shrapnel it released, shredding the top and rear of the tent to shreds. Bill being closer, his grenade landed on the centre of the tent effectively cutting it to pieces as the light machine guns and assault rifles tore holes in the rows of worshipers tossing bodies backwards and sideways from the impact of the bullets. In controlled two and three shot bursts, most of the terrorist trainees were shot down before they could get off their knees and none made it more than two or three steps away from the maelstrom of bullets raining down on them from two sides.

Three figures frantically ran out of the rear of the camp, lugging rifles with them. As agreed, Rick sighted on the one on the right and Al on the left and Rick lined up his sights on the chest of his target and tapped a three shot burst at it and then shifted to the centre target doing the same. All three went down and Rick covered them for a second, then shifted his attention to the camp once again. Al fired his high powered rifle once more at one of their targets that was still moving and there were a few more shots from the ambushers on each side, but soon there was no more movement in the camp.

Rick rose to his feet and covered by Al, made his way down the hill, rifle at his shoulder ready to fire. One look at his targets confirmed they would no longer be an issue and he cautiously continued on to the camp itself. One trooper from each side of the ambush followed his example and they made their way through each tent, ensuring no one was hiding and the camp was clear. Then waving the all clear signal, the rest of the commando came down, except for the two snipers who would be sentries. They began to drag bodies into lines facing up and took pictures of each body. While that was going on, Rick, Bill and Pat gathered papers, maps and computers. Pat began to transfer files from laptops to Ricks note book and flash drives, while Bill took pictures of every piece of paper and map. Julia came up and with Ricks help, set up the satellite equipment and they began to send the gathered data to headquarters back in Didsbury.

While that was going on, other members of the commando were wrecking the radio equipment and anything that could be used. After gathering enough ammunition that they could realistically carry, they piled the weapons and ammunition found and set them on fire, ruining them for anyone else to use. Rick had ordered that two AK74ms that the IRA trainers had been carrying, be given to the snipers to augment their sniper rifles, but the rest of the weapons in the camp were destroyed.

By noon, their work was over and after a fast hot meal, the commando retrieved their packs and were heading to the rendezvous point to meet up with their Afghan guides. It would take a couple of days to reach the spot and Rick wanted to place as much distance as he could between themselves and the ambush site as possible. They moved on through the night and by daybreak were many miles away from the at-tack site. They dug themselves in for the day and went to sleep. Two nights later and they could see the camp fires at the rendezvous place and silently moved into position around it. This group had sentries posted and it took some time to get into position without being discovered.

The camp was well positioned and not only were sentries posted, but there was a heavy machine gun manned and ready and fighting positions located within easy distance from the tents. Another sentry was guarding the horses and there appeared to be many more horses than would be required. Rick split the commando in half and they set up an ambush position on two sides of the camp. As the sun rose fully and the camp came alive, all the fighting positions and sentry posts had been marked and if this group turned out to be hostile, the commando would deal with it.

"Aw shit," Rick whispered. "Godddamn Seals."

Five men in American uniforms had made their appearance and were busy making breakfast. Rick could tell from their equipment who they were and he scanned them with his binoculars to see if he recognized any of them. He quickly confirmed that neither he nor any of his group knew them and came up with a fast plan. They were close enough to a sentry, that Rick tossed a pebble at him to gain his attention and quietly said the pass word.

"Eagles nest," he said in Russian, while noisily taking his rifle off of safe in a noise that the sentry would recognize.

"Eagles nest," he said again, a little more loudly, sighting on the man's chest.

"Bears den," the man said in badly accented Russian.

"Bill, you and your gang stay in place," Rick said over his headset in Russian. "We have some Seal visitors. Stay out of sight until I give the word."

Rick slowly stood with his arms out to his sides, almost at the feet of the shocked sentry and once he was recognized, the other four commandos rose as well, seemingly out of thin air. Taking a couple of gulps of air, the sentry hollered down to the camp and motioned for the Canadians to go to the camp. The five Canadians, in line abreast, weapons at the ready but pointed at the ground, made their way into the camp and soon were in the centre of a circle of twenty heavily armed Afghan tribesmen.

"Bear den," one bearded man said in Russian.

"Eagles Nest," Rick replied.

"Welcome, welcome," the man said, then turned to another and said something in his own language.

A great cheer went up from the group and smiles broke out and Rick and his group were subjected to much hand shaking and back ponding and were ushered to where the cook fires were and handed plates of food.

"Russians?" an American asked in that language. "Is that where you guys are from? I didn't know there were any Russians helping us out."

"No, we are originally from Ukraine," Rick said. "We are ordered to patrol this area with these allies."

"Explains the accent," the Seal said. "I knew we were negotiating with you guys. Good to have you on board. Have you run into anything?"

"No, not yet. We split up, maybe my other group has," Rick said.

"There are supposed to be some Canadian Special Forces people out here someplace. I was hoping you had spotted them. We have some new orders from my commanders for them."

"No we have not seen them. Good to know though. I will let them know if I run into them. We did hear some heavy gunfire a couple of days ago, but we are lightly armed and left the area."

"Good idea, can you show me on this map where?"

Rick pointed to the spot on the map where they had conducted the raid and the American pulled out his GPS unit and plugged in the coordinates while calling to his buddies and abruptly leaving. After conferring for a bit, he was back, while his buddies and several Afghans began to saddle horses and pack animals.

"That is the location of a big Taliban training camp," the American said. "It's a good thing you didn't stumble into them. If we spot your buddies we will send them to you."

With that, he left and soon he and his friends were on their way headed in the direction of the Taliban camp.

"You have a funny way of cooperating with your allies," the older man, who the interpreter had been talking to, said in Russian.

"When a small bird talks with an Eagle, he must always make sure he knows more than the Eagle," Rick said. "America has ten times the people we have, we are always cautious around them."

"OK Bill, you can come in once those Yanks are out of sight," Rick said, pulling his headset down from under his hat.

"Those guys ride poorly," Rick said to the Afghans. "But what can you expect from sailors? It will take them three days to cover what we just did in two."

An exclamation from another sentry as the rest of the commando rose from their positions at his feet, let Rick know the rest of the gang was coming down and the Afghan commander looked quickly behind him to see what the commotion was and made a comment about ghosts.

"Can I have a closer look at your horses? They look good from here," Rick said.

The commander stood up straighter and led Rick to the rope corral, where to Ricks quick assessment, close to eighty horses were milling about. There were four armed guards around the corral and they and the horses stopped what they were doing and watched the strangely clothed new comer approach the corral. The horses were a deep copper in colour and to the uninitiated, unremarkable. All were 16 hands high and had powerful muscles, the hooves were well trimmed and all were shod.

"These are the best horses in Afghanistan," the man said with pride. "They are descendants of a gift of thirty horses from a great Russian warrior that saved my people many years ago and we have kept the blood line pure."

Rick nodded and watched as the animals began to shift about once again.

"They will do I suppose, I am no expert," he said. "Can my horse person inspect the ones we will be riding and the equipment we will be using?"

"Pat, come over to the corral," Rick said into his microphone, "and get Julia to report in for me will you?"

Pat came up to Rick at the corral and the Afghan leader looked at her, somewhat in surprise.

"Shit Rick," Pat said, slipping into German. "Those look just like yours back home."

"Ya, I thought the same," Rick said.

"Grab one at random and put it through some paces," he said in Russian.

Quickly looking around, Pat shed her rifle and equipment, found a rope and fashioned a lasso on the end of it. Slipping under the rope corral, she began swinging the rope around her head as the horses started to mill around. With a flick of her wrist, she captured an animal, the rope about it's neck. The horse stopped immediately and she easily walked up to it, gathering up the rope as she went.

"I had heard you people were different," the Afghan said. "A black female soldier, that confirms it."

He yelled at one of the sentries, who moved to where the saddles and equipment were placed and following Pats lead, the trooper shed the rifle and equipment he was carrying and brought the saddle, saddle blanket and bridle to the edge of the coral.

"We also are different," the Afghan said nodding at the trooper. "My daughter. Are all of you Catholics or Christians?"

"Most of us are Catholics," Rick said. "One of my snipers is Muslim and one of my gunners is Jewish. My second in command is also black. If this is going to be a problem, just let us have the horses we need and we will be out of your hair."

"No, no, please," the man said placing his hand on Ricks arm. "I meant no offence. Most of us are followers of Islam, but I also have Catholics and Jews with me. But sadly, no black people. We had also heard this about your people. You make no distinction among people, as is Gods wish."

A group of Afghans had gathered around the corral as Pat deftly saddled the animal she had chosen. In a short time, she had adjusted the equipment to suit her and was motioning to the leaders daughter to open a gap in the corral. Pat had the animal outside the corral and several yards outside the camp, putting it through a number of movements before walking back up to Rick and motioning for her rifle, which Rick tossed up to her. The Afghan leader, sensing what was to occur, shouted an order to his daughter and she quickly grabbed her saddle. Another trooper caught a horse and it was quickly saddled and the woman astride it, adjusting her rifle on her back at exactly the same angle that Pat had hers. Pat nodded at her, spun her horse around and galloped out of the camp in a cloud of dust followed by the other woman.

"The current government allows this?" Rick asked.

"They have no choice," the leader said. "We supply most of the region with food and cause no problems for them. The other warlords respect us and our power and will back us if we wish. We were taught by that great leader long ago, to make no waves, to mind our own business and to fight hard when we had to. This we have done."

He went on to explain how they had supported whatever group had come into power, not by military action, but by continuing to do what they did best, supply food to areas growing poppy and other crops. They also did much like the Regiment did, funded businesses, taking small portions of the profits and not taxing their people excessively. They paid their taxes to the central government and when called upon, sent troopers to serve with whatever the central government was. His tribe had gained a reputation of being good fighters and honest and honourable and had many friends throughout the country. His area was one of the few that the Soviets had not devastated during their occupation. But, they were aware of the damage and hurt the current government was doing to the other regions of the country and would help to remove it from power.

Julia brought Rick the latest report from HQ and he showed the position on the map to the Afghan leader. The leader said he knew the place and after conferring with his men for a few minutes, they decided it would take ten days to reach the training facility, about 100 kilometres away. There would be no problem traveling in the day time, as it was normal for his troops to patrol this area. Rick asked to leave as soon as possible and soon the camp was buzzing with activity as horse packs were made up and riding horses saddled. Pat and her escort trotted back in as this was underway.

"Good animals," she said in Russian. "They will do."

"Grab a quick bite then," Rick said. "We are going to move out AS-AP."

"Julia," Rick said into his headset. "Rig up the satellite solar charges on a pack animal and get as many of our spare headset batteries charging as you can too."

"Roger," Julia said. "Home base wants an update from you ASAP. We have about an hour before we lose the satellite link."

Rick flipped up his ear piece and turned the volume up so the Afghan could hear the conversation he was about to have.

"Julia patch me in," he said.

"*Talon, Talon, this is Claw Alpha one,*" Rick said in Russian.

"*Claw Alpha One, Talon Four, sit rep,*" came loud and clear over the headset, also in Russian.

"*Talon Four, Target Alpha destroyed. One hundred three enemy KIA, no friendly casualties. Break. Positive link up with locals. Good transport. Break. Possible Ammy SF interference. Request intervention. Able to deflect Ammy at this time. Confirm air assets in place target Bravo in six days. End.*"

"*Claw Alpha one, air assets confirmed on standby for target Bravo, your call. Talon One asks if six days is enough time. Talon One will remove Ammy as a distraction for you.*"

"*Confirm Talon One, Claw on target Bravo six days.*"

"*Roger, Claw on target Bravo six days. Talon One says play safe.*"

"*God willing and the river don't rise Talon, Claw Alpha One out.*"

The Afghans were conferring rapidly in their language and Rick just looked at them and raised his eyebrow as he turned down the speaker to his headset and replaced it into his ears.

"My expert tells me these are excellent horses," Rick said loudly "Almost as good as ours. If you cannot keep up with us, we will wait for you at the target, but we will be there in five days. We are not like those Americans that just left.

"Ok you slackers," he said into the microphone. "Mount up. We're out of here."

As the Canadians rose and began slinging rifles on their backs and walking towards the horses, the Afghan leader began shouting orders and his troopers erupted into motion. By the time the Canadians had adjusted stirrups and saddles to suit them, half of the Afghans were beside them rising into saddles and a group of six spurred away. Rick nodded in approval as two went to each side and two went ahead as scouts and flankers. Settling himself into his saddle and adjusting his grip on the reins, Rick nodded at the Afghan leader, who yelled a command and the group moved out at a brisk trot in column of four.

After the first two hours, Rick stopped paying attention to his surroundings. Muscles not used to riding began to protest and he cursed himself for not training harder in the days leading up to the deployment. As they came to the overnight spot five hours after leaving, he welcomed the break and almost fell as he came down from the horse and his legs collapsed under him. Al came over to take his horse, but Rick waved him away telling him to mind his own animal. Undoing the cinch, Rick pulled the saddle off of the horses sweaty back after he had pulled a brush from the saddle bag and wiped the animal down with the saddle blanket, before draping it over the saddle. Not knowing the horse, he stood on the reins laying on the ground while he brushed the animal down, removing all the caked on dust, murmuring softly to the horse the whole time. He ran his hands expertly along the horses back and legs, feeling for hot spots or sores that would indicate an injury. Finally, after all that was done, led the horse over to the rope corral that had been laid out and removing the bridal, turned the animal loose. In typical horse fashion, the animal promptly found a spot to lay down and roll in the dust.

Returning to the spot Rick had left his saddle with the bridal across his right arm, Rick picked up the saddle and blanket and looked around to find a place to bunk down for the night. Spotting his troopers laying out their gear, he joined them, dumping the saddle on its tree and once again laying the blanket over it. His troopers had laid out a hasty fire ring of stones and breaking out a tab of fire start, got a pot of water starting to boil. Just as he was about to sit his weary bones down, the pack train arrived and with a groan, Rick joined the rest of the group in unloading the pack horses and grooming them down. Then returning to his camp spot to dump his gear beside his saddle. He unrolled his sleeping bag and took out the foamy he had rolled inside it, placing it under the bag and on top of a small tarp that he would wrap around it during the night to keep off any moisture. Feeling a tap on his shoulder, Rick turned around to see Bill with a pot in his hand and his eyebrows raised. Rummaging through his pack, Rick came up with his metal cup and Bill filled it with steaming coffee. Sipping enough to leave two inches in the cup, Rick reached back in his pack and poured enough vodka into the cup to refill it. More or less collapsing down, he leaned back against the saddle and took a deep draft of the vodka laced brew only to start violently coughing.

"Oh, did I forget to tell you?" Bill said with a large grin on his face. "I dumped some rum into the coffee."

"With a friend like you who needs enemies," Rick said after he could breath. "Just for that, you're cooking tonight."

Bill, still grinning, held out his hand and Rick rummaged through his pack again, coming up with an RME package, which he tossed at Bill who caught it and walked back to the fire. Someone in the group had found some wood and the fire was now popping away gaily. More stones had been added to the ring to make it higher and a larger pot with water in it, was draped across one corner of the stones. Bill opened Ricks MRE box, tossing the cardboard into the fire and opening the poach, he dumped the contents into the pot, while other troopers came forward and added their poaches to the pot as well.

"Ya like the boss is even going to be awake by the time this is cooked up," Al said. "Did you see how he came off that horse?"

Al mimicked, with exaggeration, how Rick had slipped off the horse and his knees buckled, then Al hobbled around holding his back groaning. The rest of the troopers howling in laughter. Rick lifted his butt, picked up a stone that had been bothering him and tossed it to bounce off Al's back.

"Just for that you're riding point tomorrow," Rick said.

Al came to attention, clicking his heels and bowed.

"Javole, mine commandant," he said in German, to more howls from his comrades.

Rick tossed another stone, this time bouncing it off Al's head.

"Sergeant Prissy," Al said, his arms stretched out in supplication to Patricia. "I wish to report abuse from a commander to his subordinate."

Patricia made as if she were writing a notice in her imaginary note book, even mimicking wetting the end of a pencil with her tongue.

"Protest noted and filed for future reference," she said, ripping the imaginary page from her imaginary note book and tossing it into the fire, with more laughter from the troopers.

"Oh, I get no respect around here," Al said in mock indignation, picking up a tin plate and spooning a pile of mixed goo into it, he walked over and handed it to Rick.

Rick rose to his feet, accepted the plate of food with his left hand and hobbled over to the troopers gathered around the fire ring. Making the sign of the cross, he knelt down on one knee and bowed his head. The other troopers quickly joined him on one knee, the Catholics among them making the sign of the cross as well.

"Bless you Father for what we are about to receive. Lord I ask you to forgive my troopers for taking the lives of Your children. Had they not, many thousands more of your servants would have been killed. We ask that you give guidance to the families of those we killed, so that they will find peace and a way to live in harmony with the rest of your children so that we no longer have to kill our fellow humans. I thank you for watching over us and allowing us to do our duty without harm and ask that you extend that protection to our new friends and allies who share the same wish for freedom and harmony as we do. Amen."

Rick made the sign of the cross again and rose to his feet. Bill nudged him in the ribs and motioned with his head to the interpreter and the Afghan leader who were standing respectfully a short distance away.

"You are welcome to join us and share our meal, bad as the food is," Rick said, motioning them forward. Bill rapidly found another two plates and spooned a helping of goo on each, handing them to the Afghans.

Gingerly sitting down, Rick crossed his legs and put the hot plate across his knees. The Afghan leader sat down beside him and took a mouthful of the goo, making a face.

"I warned you," Rick said smiling, spooning some for himself and making the same face. "It tastes worse the more you eat it, but it doesn't weigh much and is supposed to be good for you. It hasn't killed us yet, so it must be ok."

"You haven't tasted Akmed's cooking yet," the leader said smiling. "This is much better, foul as it is."

"Ha and yours is any better?" the interpreter said. "My goat cooks better than you."

"Which is why I am the leader and you are the interpreter. Now my friend, will you be able to ride the same distance or more tomorrow?"

"To much time behind a desk I am afraid," Rick said. "I will be fine. I would like to put one of my people with your flankers and scouts from now on if you don't mind."

"Yes, this was also on my mind," the leader said.

"I am Bashir Khan," he said, sticking out his hand to Rick. "My people have decided I make a good leader."

"Rick," Rick said shaking the preferred hand. "The unfortunate leader of this group of ungrateful misfits."

"Hey speak for yourself, misfit," Bill said. "I'll have you know my mother doesn't appreciate you calling me a misfit. Hi, I'm Bill, this ya-hoos second in command."

"So, you had a victory over our common enemy?" Bashir said.

"Not much of a victory," Rick said. "Just as we planned, they came out and lined up in nice neat rows to pray and we cut them down."

"Ah, just as the Prophet Mohammed said in the Koran," Basher said. "You will find no such slackness among my people."

"Yes we saw that," Rick said. "I hope you understand that I only wish to have my people riding with your scouts to provide radio comms and to gain familiarity with your people. It is in no way reflective of your abilities. Your people seem very well trained and professional."

"Yes, I understand this. You already strike us as much different from the American and Soviet advisors we have had in the past," Bashir said. "I was about to ask you to send your people out for the same reason. Your horse expert tells my daughter that you have had little sleep for the last few days. I will not take up much of your time tonight. Might I suggest you get some rest? It will be a rough couple of days to come."

With that, Bashir and Akmed finished their meals and coffee. Shaking hands once again, they walked back to their part of the camp, leaving the Canadians to their meals. Rick told Bill to post two sentries on two hour shifts and that he would take the last shift, shuffled over to his bedroll and collapsed into it, falling asleep as he hit the ground.

Rick woke to the sun poking over the horizon and into his eyes and the sound of troops and horses milling about. Getting his bearings, he stood and stretched the kinks out of his back in the cold morning air, seeing horses being saddled and packs being loaded. Bill walked up with a plate of steaming food and a cup of coffee and gave them to Rick.

"What the hell?" Rick burst out in English. "I told you I would take the last sentry shift Bill. You let me sleep through!"

"Well, it's like this..." Bill said.

"No, I gave you a direct order and you disregarded it!" Rick was warming up to his displeasure. "In the field, in a war zone, is no time to piss around with silly games!"

"Officer on deck!" Bill blurted, out looking over Rick's shoulder in Russian.

"Warrant Officer Rick, a moment of your time?" Bashir said in British accented English, motioning Rick to follow him.

The two men walked to the edge of the camp where Bashir stopped and looked out over the valley they would be riding down shortly.

"Warrant Officer, I ordered your troops to stand down last night and to let you rest. I am the ranking officer in this little group and while I will take suggestions from your people to heart, I make the orders here. When we return, you will apologize to Warrant Officer Bill."

Bashir turned around and looked directly into Ricks eyes.

"You are no longer only ten troopers alone. We are now thirty five. My second in command will draw up a sentry schedule that will include your people, but not tonight or the next night. You and your people need the rest. You have been constantly on the move for three days with little rest. We need you and your people to be fully functional.

"Secondly, while I am in fact the ranking officer, you my friend are the actual leader. I need you well rested and your mind functioning as well as possible. You will not stand watch, or prepare meals or set up camp. We have people for that. A commander has no time for those things, it is time you learned that. Your people already know you can and are able and willing to do everything you order them to do. They need your mind more than they need you doing guard duty. Is that clear?"

"Yes sir," Rick said.

"Good," Bashir said. "Come, I will introduce you to my nephew."

Whistling, he waved over a young man. He was about six feet tall and was wearing western style cloths and boots, with a cloth baseball cap on his head.

"This is Corporal Kahlil Kahn, my nephew," Bashir said. "He will be your batman. He is fluent in English and Russian and if he lives and does well, he will be promoted to a lieutenant once we return home. Now, both of you get out of my sight. I want to be on the move within the hour."

"Sir!" both men said and left Bashir looking at their backs shaking his head as they walked away.

"Warrant Officer Rick," Kahlil said. "I took the liberty of saddling your horse and moving my riding and pack animals to your camp. I will have your equipment loaded a few moments after we return."

"Very well," Rick said, as they approached a smirking Bill.

"Alright you smirking smart ass," Rick said. "You're off the hook, this time and that's the most apology you will get from me as ordered by the boss. This is Kahlil, he is my new batman and will be tagging along with us. Now get your ass in gear and get on the move before I really get pissed off. And where is my coffee?"

"Yes me Lord, thank you me Lord, whatever your say me Lord," Bill said, making a mock bow while handing Rick another cup of coffee.

"Now Kahlil, you will have to pardon his lordship, he is right cranky in the mornings until he gets his coffee."

"Yes, I have noticed that these big shots are like that," Kahlil said. "My uncle is the same."

Rick took a sip of his coffee and swore as the hot cup touched his lips. Then shook his head as the two men moved away. They were immediately replaced by Julia who reported that the solar chargers were in place on the pack horses and charging already and that comms were up and functioning. HQ had nothing new to report, other than the Seals were closing in on the last ambush site and were still trying to make contact with them. Al was next reporting that the troops were all in good shape and ready to go, a rotation of scouts had been set up and that no, Rick was not on it. Patricia reported that the horses were all fine. Akmed arrived and reported that they were ready and after Ricks request, reported that like the Canadians, they were armed with AK74ms and RPKms. In addition, they had one RPK, several RPG launchers and sufficient rockets and a light mortar. By this time Bill and Kahlil had returned with the horses and Rick told Akmed to inform Bashir they were ready to leave. The three designated scouts mounted and joined the three Afghan scouts, swiftly leaving the camp heading for their positions on the flanks and the point. Rick slung his rifle over his back and made sure all his personal equipment and ammunition were in place, before checking the horse and making minor adjustments to its equipment and he mounted. Riding the short distance to where his pack horse was, he was about to take up the halter lead when Kahlil took it first.

"No, sir, that is my job sir," Kahlil said. He led the animal to where his own pack horse was and deftly tied his pack horses lead to Rick's horses tail before mounting his own horse and walking it back to where the rest of the Canadians were waiting. One less thing to worry about, thought Rick and in short order the order to move out was given and the whole group moved off at a trot.

After an hour or so, Rick dropped back to ride next to Kahlil and asked him, in Russian, how he had learned to speak these languages. Kahlil's Russian was also flawless. He told Rick that they were all trained to speak those languages. Some spoke better than others, but all understood. Some, the ones that were slated to become officers, like himself, were sent to England and Russia for a year for further studies and in Russia, they were trained on military weapons and tactics as well. And that no, as far as he knew, no one spoke German. As they were in the middle of the group and were not trying to conceal their conversation, all the Canadians heard it and nodded to Rick when he looked at them, to indicate they had understood.

"Be advised," Rick heard over his ear piece as Julia reported to everyone. "Our friends are all fluent in Russian and English."

Rick next rode next to Patricia.

"Pat," he said. "Strike up a conversation with Bashir's daughter and find out how well these horses are trained. Are they just normal riding horses, or cavalry trained horses and what kind of cavalry training do the horses and troops have."

"Right," Patricia said, she dropped back in the formation to ride beside Bashir's daughter and soon they were in deep conversation. All that handled, Rick settled down to the mind numbing ride and let the hours pass.

It was getting dark when they finally reached the spot chosen to camp for the night. Rick was sore, but today did not collapse as he dismounted and he waved Kahlil away, unsaddling and brushing down his horse himself. His troopers set up camp faster this night and by the time Rick dropped his horse off and his saddle down, Kahlil had a coffee ready for him. Taking the coffee, he turned on his GPS unit and while it was finding their position, he pulled his map from his leg pocket and spread it out, taking a deep draft of the rum laced coffee.

"Corporal, are you trying to make me an alcoholic?" Rick asked. "I thought you Muslims were forbidden alcohol?"

"Oh yes sir, we are," Kahlil said. "But we are allowed for medicinal purposes. I have found that Rum and coffee relaxes the muscles after a long ride."

"You have a point there corporal, but next time, put half what you put in this time will you?"

"Yes sir and sir, the Colonel would like you to have dinner with him tonight."

"You don't call me sir Corporal, I work for a living," Rick said. "You call me Warrant or Mr."

"Yes Warrant, I will inform the Colonel, you will be with him shortly."

The GPS unit had locked into their position and Rick plotted it on his map, turned it off and folding it up again, put it and his map back in his pants cargo pocket. Julia had already erected her coms aerials and was writing a message down and Bill was wondering Ricks way with Patricia beside him. Rick motioned to the coffee pot and both troopers poured themselves a good measure, Patricia coughing at the potent mixture.

"They like their coffee a little stronger than us," Rick said.

"Shit, I thought Muslims didn't do booze," Bill said. "Maybe that's why."

"Something about it's ok for medicinal purposes," Rick said. "I told him to lighten it up the next time. What did you find out Pat?"

"It would seem that they have much the same training as we do," Pat said. "Minus the armoured vehicle training we have. It seems that this famous Russian they keep talking about had a major impact on them and they modelled their training after his methods. The horses are all fully cavalry trained, even the pack horses. They have about a thousand active duty troops and about another five thousand in reserve. Women as well as men are allowed to serve, but it is mandatory for the men. Most of the women choose to serve though and a few of them are good enough to be front line troops, much like us. There are ten women here. Six are medical people and the rest have combat specialties."

"Our friend Bashir," Bill said. "Is actually a general and is the clan's headman."

"Ya well we will let the charade stand until he chooses otherwise," Rick said. "It doesn't really matter at this point."

"Yo Gadget," Julia said. "Any coffee left for the poor grunt that has to do all the work?"

"Holy shit that's strong!" she said after taking a gulp. "Ok, so the General has retired, the Master Warrant is now the General and you my friend are now the Master Warrant. Congrats."

"Ah come on," Rick said shaking his head. "I don't need that shit."

"To bad, so sad and you're buying the drinks whenever we get to civilization," Julia said.

"Well at least they didn't make you an officer, yet," Bill said.

"Shit that would really take the cake," Rick said. "I'd have to become a collage boy then."

"Warrant, the Colonel says anytime you are ready," Kahlil said. "And Warrant Bill is to come too. Also, Sergeant Julia and Sergeant Pat are to dine with our female troopers and the rest of your troops with ours."

"Well isn't that nice?" Rick said. "Ok Corporal, pass the word to the guys and as soon as Sergeant Julia finishes her report we will be right with the Colonel."

"The Americans are putting pressure on Battalion to commit, but as usual we are resisting," Julia said. "It has been confirmed that the bounties on those yahoos we hit the other day have pretty much paid for this operation and all of us have nice bonuses waiting for us. Battalion has told the Yanks we are operating in the dark and will not break radio silence for another five days to a week. That should get the Seals off our case for a bit. No air support for a few more days and that's about it."

"Ok, morning meeting during breakfast and I want to be ready to rock at daybreak," Rick said. "Julia have your sat feed ready for then. Let's adjourn for dinner then shall we?"

"Why of course Me Lord," Julia said. "Patricia dear, do you think my frock is good enough for tonight's party?"

"But of course Dear Julia, your attire is as always impeccable," Patricia said, as she took Julia's arm and they began to sashay toward where the Afghans had set up camp. "I do wish My Lord would give us some warning for the next party. My nails are in such a mess."

"Um, um" Bill said. "I do love the way she swings those hips of hers."

"Ya thanks bud," Rick said. "That's all I need to hear, you two rutting like goats tonight."

"No fear of that bud," Bill said. "I ain't Super Man like you. My ass is way to sore for that."

"Ah Master Warrant Rick and Warrant Bill, welcome," Bashir said. "Come sit, some tea?"

Bill and Rick sat on the rug placed outside Bashir's tent. There were four other men present and Bashir introduced them as his subordinate officers. The two Canadians shook hands all around and settled down to light conversation as the meal was presented and eaten. The Colonel proved to be a good host and soon the group was laughing as he explained some humorous incidents from his past. Soon the simple meal was finished and as the after dinner coffee was poured, the Colonel became serious.

"I noticed you have a GPS," he said.

"Yes sir," Rick said and he pulled out his map and handed it to the colonel. "We made fifty K today and I make it roughly twenty to the next target. If you don't mind sir, I would like to be on the move at daybreak and have a camp set up a kilometre or two from the target by noon."

"Yes, I know a suitable spot," the Colonel said. "We should make it by noon without issue. I shall send an advanced party out before we leave. You will send one of your troopers with them please.

"You will want to hit them as soon as we are able then?"

"If you don't mind Colonel," Rick said. "I would like to observe them for a day or so. Then I can make a recommendation for an attack."

"This camp will be like the last one you attacked," one of the officers said. "We will have no problem with them. Why wait?"

"I need to see the strength of the enemy. The layout of their positions and possible escape routes for us if it all goes wrong," Rick said. "Unlike you, I have no reinforcements and am a very long way from resupply. I haven't lost any people yet and I don't want to. I have learned the hard way not to underestimate my opponents."

"But you run the risk of being exposed," the officer said. "It is better to hit them fast."

"I see the wisdom of your plan," the colonel said. "Tell me Mr. Rick, how long did you observe us before making your presence known?"

"From just about sunset the day before," Rick said.

"Captain, did you see how he had his troops deployed when they made their presence known? They were right under our noses and could easily have killed us all. No I think we will use his plan. Perhaps you could take some of my better people with you? We have much to learn I think. Captain, you will accompany Mr. Rick tomorrow."

"Colonel, I am going to be relying on your people to provide us with a number of egress routes and rendezvous points," Rick said. "I think we will be ok on the assault, as the Captain pointed out, they don't know we are here yet. But I also think that this being the second camp to be attacked, we might be in for a rough time afterwards."

"Yes, we know this area quite well," the Colonel said. "I agree it would be better to be far away as soon as possible after the attack. Good then, I will have my people work on that and I think we should say goodnight if we are to leave so early tomorrow."

"That was a good idea Hakim," the colonel said as the Canadians walked away. "He is good that one, for being so young. The Americans would have made you feel foolish."

"As would have the Russians," Hakim said. "You notice he asked, not ordered and explained his reasons. I think these people are better than the Spetznaz I trained with. Yes you were correct, we didn't detect them until they wanted us to see them."

Chapter Five

Hakim glanced over to his right where Rick was laying. The man had hardly moved since they had arrived on the hill top as the grey light of dawn had just began to show grey on the eastern horizon. Rick had his binoculars propped on a small pack so they were at his eye level and now, as he had at intervals throughout the day, he pulled his right hand slowly from under his chin and wrote something on a piece of paper he had clipped to a covered clip board. Once he was finished, Rick slowly placed his hand back under his chin. At one point in the now hot day, Hakim had observed a large black spider crawl onto the back of Rick's neck and watched as Rick had used the same slow movement to pluck the insect from his neck and quietly flick it away from himself.

Looking to his right, Hakim once again tried to spy where the other observation team was and once again failed to spot them. He was sore and stiff from the inactivity of the day, his stomach had started to growl and he had but a mouthful of water left in his water bottle. The sun was almost gone now, the targets were all moving to their barracks, yet still the man next to him made no movement to leave. Once again writing something down after he had observed something of interest to him. Several times during the day, Hakim had found himself falling asleep and had received a nudge on his ankle from Rick's boot each time he had. Not a whisper had passed between them all day. The last person in the camp had finished their last cigarette and the lights had all gone out in all the buildings and after an hour, Rick finally gathered his clip board, keyed the mic on his head set twice and began to belly crawl backwards down the hill they had been on observing the camp. Once they were down at the bottom, and out of sight of the camp, Rick stood and stretched. Reaching to his water bottle, he unscrewed the lid and took a deep draft, then passed the bottle to Hakim.

"Not to worry, I have another," Rick whispered. Then he reached into a pocket and pulled out two power bars and gave one to Hakim. Putting his binoculars around his neck, Rick shouldered his rifle and unwrapped the bar as he began to walk.

He chuckled softly and said, "I thought your stomach was going to betray us a few times there."

"Like yours was being so quiet too," Hakim said, chuckling himself.

"I once broke up a clever SAS ambush like that," Rick said. "There were five of them and we had not spotted them. Then one of them drew our attention when his stomach growled and we were able to determine their positions and how many of them there were just from that one tiny noise."

A few minutes later, as Hakim was reaching into his left breast pocket for his pack of cigarettes, Rick grabbed his hand and going to one knee, pulled his rifle from his shoulder and aimed it to the left. Hakim quickly followed suit, looking over the sights into the darkness, he heard Rick blow into his mike twice.

"Ya it's us," came a voice in the darkness. "I told the kid you'd find us if he lit that smoke."

Two dark figures joined them from the left and Rick stood and shouldered the rifle.

"*Charley six, Charley one,*" Rick said.

"*Charley six, Charley one and Charley five RTB. ETA one hour, out.*" Rick said. "Ok gents, smoke em if you want. I don't think anybody but us is out here now."

Only Hakim pulled out his cigarettes and as he lit it, Rick closed his eyes so as not to destroy his night vision.

"So you have seen and made a plan?" Hakim asked.

"We will make our report to your commander and go from there," Rick said.

The rest of the trip was made in silence. The moon and stars gave enough light so they could see well enough not to trip on obvious obstacles and sooner than an hour later, Rick called a halt.

"Charley six, Charley one," Rick said. *"Charley six, we are at the perimeter. I would like not to be perforated. I am dehydrated enough already."*

Ten yards away a dark figure rose and waved them in.

"Christ, I could smell you guys for the last five minutes," Bill said. "Bad ops security Rick."

"Long day," Rick said. "The boys deserved a smoke. Bashir still up?"

"Ya he's waiting for you," Bill said.

"Gather the gang and meet us at his place," Rick said and he and his three companions headed in the direction of Bashir's tent.

"Ah you have returned," Bashir said. "Come, I have hot food and drink waiting inside."

As they ate, there was no talk of the observation mission and as a group, the other nine Canadians entered the tent accompanied by two of Bashir's officers.

"So corporal, what did you see?" Rick asked. "Take your time and tell us everything. Nothing is unimportant."

The corporal, who had been with Al, described the building layout, the number of people he had seen and what they had done during the time they had been watching them. After he had finished, Rick asked Hakim the same question and Hakim went through the same process. Rick then looked at Al and nodded. He gave almost the same report as the corporal, giving a more accurate count of the people, how many were placed on guard during the day and approximated distances to the buildings and the guard posts.

Rick pulled out his note pad and began reading off what he had written there.

"First of all good job guys," Rick said. "Corporal, we could not see those five women you saw from where we were. Also, you did not see the four we saw from our position. There are one hundred fifty seven people down there including the women. The four women at our position were armed and are part of the officer core. The main group go into the main mess hall at about 08:00 and ten officers go into the small east building at about the same time. There are no sentries posted until after they have eaten. There are four sentry positions located one at each corner of the camp and a large caliber RPK in the centre, not manned but loaded. The small building to the west appears to be the woman's quarters as well as the communications centre. The building to the north, the men's barracks and the small one to the east, the officer's barracks and mess hall. I have sketched out the layout and approximate distances to the targets as well as my suggestion for our positions and targets for the RPG and mortar teams."

Rick laid the sketches he had made on the table and stepped back, letting Bashir and Hakim look at them. The Afghans had a quick look and a discussion, then Bashir looked at Rick.

"When do we call in the air support?" he asked "And what targets shall we give them?"

"I think we can handle this on our own," Rick said. "We can't have air support for another three days. We can hit the bad guys tomorrow when they sit down for breakfast. If we wait until we have air support, we are asking to be discovered or for things to change. I recommend hitting them tomorrow."

"I agree," Hakim said. "They are not so many and have sloppy security. That may change at any time."

"Good," Bashir said. "This is what we will do. It is a good plan. Warrant Rick, disperse your people among mine. I will leave three behind to mind the camp and the horses. Can you leave them a radio? Placing six, three to each side of the ambush to catch possible escapees, I had not thought of. This we will do also, put one of your people with each team please. So go now, get some rest we leave very early."

There was little left of the buildings after the attack. What the mortars, RPGs and machine guns had been left undamaged, the fires they had started, finished. The few of the enemy that had escaped the buildings had been cut down by the massed assault rifles before they had gone more than a few steps. None had survived and none had fired back. Once again the bodies were laid out in rows and those that were recognizable were photographed. A safe found in the officers' quarters was hauled out before the fire in the building became to hot and yielded a large number of documents written in Arabic. These too were photographed. The relatively undamaged barracks and communications building were plundered and yielded more weapons and ammunition. The radio equipment that was usable was taken, then both buildings were set on fire. The Afghans now had an additional large caliber machine gun and four light caliber ones. All of the plunder was loaded onto pack horses and within two hours, the raiders were on the move at a fast trot.

They had put thirty kilometres away before Bashir called a halt for the day. The sun was going down and the rest area was flush with grass for the horses and a small stream wound through the hills to each side. Julia told Rick that she would have comms available within a half an hour and Kahlil had Rick's coffee, this time with less rum, ready by the time he walked over to where Julia had set up.

"Data has been sent Gadget," Julia said. "Battalion has cancelled target Charley and has given us new coordinates for another target."

Rick pulled out his GPS and punched in the new coordinates and swore. "Get me battalion on net." He said. "And send someone for Bashir."

"Eagle base this is Charley One. Confirm coordinates over," Rick said and swore again as the same coordinates were given.

"What's the target?"

"We have reports of high value targets hidden in caves located in that region. Higher command has ordered us to patrol, search and destroy the area."

"It will take us at least two, possibly three weeks to travel that far, is Eagle One aware of that?"

"Charley One, Eagle One," Rick heard his father say. *"American President contacted the PM and personally requested our involvement. They are aware of the time frame Charley One, but we are still the best and closest force available."*

"We are going to need resupply," Rick said. *"We have rations only enough for the next week."*

"Air drop of supplies is being arranged right now," Paul said. *"So far NATO nations are on board and the Americans are working hard on a UN resolution which should happen shortly. What are you going to need?"*

"We have ten foxtrot and twenty five other ranks," Rick said. *"We also have one hundred transport. Ammunition is not an issue at this point. Local water is plentiful at this time."*

"Roger. Ten foxtrot and twenty five other ranks, one hundred transport. Ammunition and water not required. Report back in two days your anticipated coordinates for the drop. It will take us a couple of days to get it to you. Interesting group you seem to have gathered."

"You could say that. Not what we were expecting that's for sure. Try and keep the Yanks off our case as long as you can Eagle One."

"Roger, CIA is getting anxious. Keep safe kid."

"Roger Eagle One, Kid is definitely keeping head down. Charley One out."

"Crap, another month of travel," Rick said tossing the mic to Julia.

"Do you know this area?" Rick asked Bashir, showing him on the map.

"Yes, we operated out of there against the Russians," Bashir said. "Rumour has it that the bad guys big shots are hiding in the cave complexes there. We could make it in a week or so. But we would lose a lot of animals and would be not be in good shape our selves."

"I told them three weeks tops," Rick said. "I don't want to run into any ambushes or populated areas and at the end, we need to be a functioning force."

"Supplies are going to be a problem," Bashir said.

"They are going to air drop to us," Rick said. "Five days from now where do you think we can be and can they drop it to us there."

"Yes there is a good spot just here," Bashir pointed on the map. "I will send three men to make sure all is good. I think also, that I will have remounts sent to this location here and will send another three men home to make that happen."

Bashir also said that while the local populations would have no problem with them, it was still best to be prepared for action at any time. Not all of the population were for change and in fact some of the local war lords might want to challenge them for their weapons and animals. The fact, that unlike the Americans and the Russians before them, Rick's group not wearing body armour would actually be helpful. Also their beards were starting to grow, which would also be helpful. They rode as good, or better, than most Afghans did, from a distance they would pass any casual observers glance as being part of Bashir's group.

"Uniform Kilo, this is Alpha Charley Six," Rick heard over his head set. It was the SEAL team again.

"Yes Alpha Charley Six," Rick said in Russian. *"What can the democratic free forces do for you today?"*

"We need a sit rep ASAP," the SEAL said.

"We ourselves have seen nothing," Rick said. *"We did hear much firing to the west of us yesterday. Lots of automatic and mortar fire, followed by a large amount of smoke. Again, unfortunately we have limited resources and must keep a low profile. Wait one minute, ah, here are the coordinates where we heard the action."*

"Ok, we will check it out, Alpha Charley Six out."

"I wonder Alpha Charley Six. Would you be so kind as to give us a control phrase? Just in case one of your very capable jet fighter pilots happens to see us and mistake us for the bad guys?"

"Just say Uniform Kilo when queried on Guard Channel, Alpha Charley Six out."

"I wonder, do the Americans know how much they sound like Russians?" Bashir asked. "The accent is terrible, but the air of superiority is the same."

"Like my grandfather said, Bashir," Rick said. "The ant does not tell the elephant what to do. For the most part they are good people. We work with them a lot. I would say the upper class is better than the Russian one though."

"Good analogy," Bashir said. "Yes we found the regular Russian soldiers were good guys for the most part, crude, but good guys. The officers and higher ups though. Different story."

"Well, I have to clean my weapon and reload my clips and it will be an early morning," Rick said. "So I bid you good night. Your people did well today."

"You as well Warrant Rick," Bashir said. *And if you live long enough you will make your people a good leader one day,* he thought.

Chapter Six

Damn, Paul thought. That kid has hit the jackpot again. He had just finished looking at the pictures and identification papers of the dead terrorists from the last raid in Afghanistan. Once again some top Taliban and Al-Qaida organizers had been on site, as well as a number of people on the most wanted lists of several countries. The bounties from this one raid would amount to almost three million dollars. In addition to paper records that had been photographed, there were a large number of computer files that Julia had extracted from laptop computers and flash drives they had recovered. Al-Qaida had suffered a severe blow, just from this one raid and so far they didn't even know it yet. To top it off, three Pakistani intelligence officers and ten Pakistani troops had been killed as well. What the NATO leaders would do with that hot potato, Paul did not know. Pakistan was supposed to be their ally in this war.

"General, your meeting is in twenty minutes," Paul aid said.

"Ya ok," Paul said. "Have all this intelligence sent to CICIS, CIA and MI6. I want our code crackers and Arabic translators working on it as well. Next, we need to put together rations and supplies for thirty five troopers, ten of whom are female. High quality horse feed for one hundred horses and ten more radios, night vision goggles, batteries and solar charging packs. This needs to be ready for air drop to Afghanistan in two days. Make sure there is some fresh food included and maybe some letters from family and friends. Everything has to be able to be packed by horse. Then we need to get it over there. We need to do that every five days after that."

"Yes sir, I'll get right on it."

Two weeks ago, Paul had received a letter from the Indian Affairs Office in Ottawa and the Chief Inspectors Office of the RCMP, requesting a meeting for this morning. No other information had been provided. All he knew was that keeping away from bureaucrats and political nonsense had always been a policy with the Regiment and dealing with the Indian Affairs Department was always dicey. He had the Regimental, company and colony lawyers on standby just in case.

Paul pored himself another cup of coffee from the always ready pot in his office and went over his uniform tunic to make sure everything was in order. Unlike other regiments, the Regiment, unless they were actually in the field, wore the dark green Canadian Army official uniform. They had no need to show off their prowess by wearing the new camouflage patterned uniforms that had become popular with other units. As usual, his aides had his uniform impeccable, not a spec of dust or tarnish was evident and today, all of his ribbons were attached in a broad swath above the breast pocket.

"General," his aid said, poking his head in the door. "A convoy with about a hundred Mounties, tribal police and civilians in vehicles just crossed into the colony and are headed for the base."

"Right," Paul said. "Alert the gate and have them pass everyone through on my authority and provide an escort to the officer's mess. Then, send my regards to the Colonels and ask that they join me, with their aids at the O mess entrance in ten minutes. Ask Warrant Smid to provide light refreshments for one hundred plus guests and to close the O mess to everything but us. Finally, you and my office staff are to accompany me at the meeting. I want notes kept of everything said."

Eight minutes later, Paul was standing at the entrance to the Officers Mess and his staff were arranging themselves in a line, pulling at tunics and squaring away berets. They were joined two minutes later by Emily and Elizabeth and their aides, all dressed in their dark green uniforms, ribbons and awards in clear view, aids cords draped through epaulets. They arranged themselves in front of Paul's staff in a line and after Paul gave Emilie's aide a grim look at the loose tie she had, the whole group hurriedly went over their uniforms to make sure they were ship shape. Warrant Smid rushed out hurriedly buttoning his tunic, came to attention and saluted Paul who acknowledged the gesture with a wave in the general direction of his forehead and thanked the Warrant for his indulgence at such short notice. After informing the general that all would be in readiness and seeing the convoy of vehicles approaching, saluted once again and sprinted back into the Officers Mess.

Paul took two steps forward and assumed the position of parade rest, his feet shoulder width apart and hands clasped in the small of his back. The two Colonels flanked him on each side one step behind him and a fast stomp of feet, told Paul the assembled troopers had also assumed the at ease position.

The approaching convoy was indeed impressive. An armed, highly polished G wagon headed the procession, followed by the guard officer in his G Wagon. Behind that were an RCMP cruiser, an Alberta Sheriffs cruiser and a Tribal Police cruiser. Behind those vehicles were an assortment of government vehicles and private SUVs, then another Tribal Police, Alberta Sheriffs and RCMP cruiser and another armed G wagon. Paul nodded in approval as the gunners and the G wagons took over watch positions, training their C6s to cover the perimeter. As Mounties, Sheriffs and Tribal Police piled out of cruisers in their official uniforms to run to the civilian vehicles and open doors, the guard officer, his pistol on the chest of his body armour and buckling his Kevlar helmet on, marched up to Paul and saluted. Paul smartly returned the salute and thanked the lieutenant for the escort. While the civilians were sorting themselves out in the frigid early November air, the Mounties assembled in a line, hurriedly joined by the Sheriffs and Tribal Police on each flank. Each contingent was wearing their official uniforms. The Mounties in their dark brown tunics and brimmed hats, the Sheriffs and Police in their dark blues. Each had their officer or officers in the case of the Mounties ranged in front of their lines. Paul noticed that the lowest rank of the RCMP was a single corporal, the rest were all Sergeants. The Inspector of K Division stepped in front of the formation, called them to attention and had them salute.

"Troop Attention!" Paul barked. "Troop Salute!"

The battalions people crashed to attention and as one provided the hand salute to the assembled Policemen.

Paul put his people back at ease and stepped forward to shake the hand of the Inspector.

"Good to see you again Jean," Paul said. "If I may suggest, perhaps Sergeant Macintyre could escort your people to the Junior Ranks Mess? He knows where it is."

Sergeant Macintyre was in charge of the Didsbury RCMP detachment and had spent many an hour off duty with the Regiments non-commissioned officers, swapping war stories over a beer and a steak in the mess.

"Major!" Paul said to his aide. "Please escort the other gentlemen into the mess and ask Warrant Smid to call over to the junior ranks mess and have them expect some visitors immediately."

Paul's aide gestured to the two RCMP and one each of the Tribal Police and Alberta Sheriffs officers to follow him and they entered the mess as the other aides and Paul's staff followed them inside. Then the civilians approached and the Inspector introduced Paul to the Federal and Provincial representatives, both heads of their Alberta departments and the Chief of the Cree Federation, who impatiently remarked on how cold it was and shouldn't they go inside. Paul noticed that he and his aides were smartly dressed in expensive suits and that the other six men with him were dressed in well-made but serviceable business attire. He also noticed that they were not introduced. The man and his aides then bulled their way into the mess. Paul looked at the other six representatives, one of whom shrugged his shoulders and they meekly followed the grand chief into the mess. Paul waited until all the guests were ushered inside, then he and his people filed in.

The tables had been hastily arranged into a square around the dance floor and the Grand Chief and his entourage had already taken position of one of the sides, himself in the centre and already calling for a drink. The civilian delegation took another group of tables to one side of the native delegation and the policemen the other side, leaving the side opposite the Grand Chief for the Regiment, which also had its backs to the door. All of the civilians were seated while the Regiments people arranged themselves at their side of the room, more tables being hurriedly brought to accommodate Paul's staff who were setting up laptops and writing pads. When all was ready Paul sat and the uniformed personnel followed suit.

Starting with Paul, servers poured red wine into wine glasses and put them in front of each person, the Grand Chief taking a deep draught of his the minute he grabbed hold of it. When each person in the room had their glass in front of them, Paul took his glass in his right hand and stood. The Regiments officers and the Police officers stood, followed by the civilians. The six tribal elders also rose, followed belatedly by the Grand Chief and his people.

The most junior lieutenant on Paul's staff raised his glass to the portrait of the queen on the wall. "To the Queen!" he said and drained his glass. All the officers and civilians followed suit and Paul sat.

"Thank you lieutenant, well done," Paul said as the wine glasses were all refilled. "Welcome to our home gentlemen. How may we help you?"

"Are you the Earl?" the Grand Chief demanded. "We were assured the Earl would be here. Otherwise this meeting has no meaning."

Paul noticed Elizabeth's right hand clench and he put his left over it as she made to rise. "Sir, the third Earl of Didsbury has died and the fourth Earl has yet to be confirmed by Her Majesty. I am Ataman of the Andrea Host and Her Majesty has appointed myself, Colonel Bekenbaum and Colonel von Hoaelde as regents empowered to act in his name. In any case, the Earl is currently engaged overseas on an important military mission on behalf of the Dominion of Canada and Her Majesty and would be unavailable."

"General Bekenbaum," the K Division Inspector said. "As I am sure you are aware, there is a gang and crime problem in the Ermineskin and

Samson First Nations. The Elders asked their councils to provide a solution to the problem and they in turn asked the Minister for some possible solutions, who then approached us. Knowing of your situation here and the success you have achieved with your young people, I suggested a possible solution. Indian Affairs and the councils agreed and here we are."

"General," the Federal man said. "I was tasked by the Ministry to ascertain whether or not it would be possible under the terms specified under Treaty Six to implement this plan and delved into the history of the Earldoms of Didsbury and Olds and found that indeed, your charters were used as a template for the drafting of Treaty Six. Your historical backgrounds are very similar to those of the First Nations and yet where you have prospered, the First Nations have not. The Ministry then determined that perhaps you could impart some of your knowledge to guide the Samson and Ermineskin First Nations."

"This is all Hogwash!" the Grand Chief said rising from his chair. "More bullshit talking and Whiteman stalling. The real issue here is why the government doesn't give us more money! We can fix our own problems!"

This time Elizabeth rose before Paul could stop her, but once again he put his hand over her clenched fist and motioned her to sit.

"Gentlemen, I must apologize for Colonel von Hoaedles outburst," Paul said. "It has been some years since she has been involved in touchy negotiations and like the Grand Chief, she is used to having ultimate authority."

"Ah, this is all bullshit and a colossal waste if my time!" the Grand Chief said and followed by his two aides, angrily left the room.

"Major," Paul said to his aide. "Please inform Warrant Smid that those three gentlemen are to be barred from this room and inform the Provost Officer of the day to provide an armed guard and to escort those three gentlemen from the base and the colony."

"Now, gentlemen," Paul said, addressing the six band council members that had stayed in the room. "Do you wish to continue this meeting?"

"Yes sir we do," the eldest said. "Unlike the Grand Chief, we have had many dealings with your people in the past and you have always treated us fairly and with respect. You signed your treaty and established your reserve but a few years before ours, yet you have done extremely well and we have not. Your people live well, you have good schools and hospitals. You are respected not only in Canada but all over the world. Our people live in poverty and crime. We want to break that cycle. In the past we were to proud to ask for help, now we come on bended knee."

"I presume this is related to the latest incident at the Samson Reserve?" Paul asked. "The one where the infant was killed in her crib by a drive by shooting?"

Every civilian in the room nodded their heads.

"First, let me tell you that we have our share of crime and drunkenness, like every other society," Paul said. "The difference is that we take these things serious and if found guilty, the perpetrator is handed over to the civilian authorities and must suffer the consequences. If the offence is serious enough, the perpetrator is expelled from the Host and the Colony and has no recourse. And I can tell you, if something like that drive by shooting ever happened here, I would have more than one shooting to investigate and would likely never find the second shooters."

"This happens with us as well," the Elder said. "The difference is, we don't want them to happen in the first place. Our police and the RCMP are trying, but it seems to be getting worse. The more money we throw at it the worse it gets."

"What would you have us do?" Paul asked.

"We would like to set up an Army Cadet program," another elder said. "We believe that perhaps some discipline at a young age will help."

"You are most likely correct," Paul said. Now he was all but ignoring the other civilians in the room. "The problem will still be there though. What have your young people to look forward to when they grow up? You still have no jobs for them. If they leave the reserve, they are ostracized by their peers. They have no life skills to deal with the outside world."

"Again we would like you to help us in this matter," a third elder said. "Many times in the past we have tried to start businesses but failed, where your people have not. We would learn your secrets."

Paul thought for a few moments and then nodded his head. "Gentlemen," he said, addressing the civilians and police officials. "If you don't mind I would like the Colonels and I to talk directly with the band elders privately. Please ask for anything you need from the Warrant or his staff. Elders, if you would be kind enough to join the Colonels and I in our private board room? Major see that we have some coffee and food brought to the board room and make yourself and the Colonels aids available should we need you."

The first thing Paul did when he entered the board room was to take off his tunic and toss it on a chair, followed by the loosening of his tie and opening the top button of his shirt. Then he sat down on a randomly selected chair and motioned everyone else to join him. Everyone else followed his example taking off jackets and losing ties, happy to be out of the constraining garments. Once the coffee was poured and the large pot left in the room. Paul began again.

"All right, all of us know each other here so we can cut out the bullshit," Paul said. "First thing, are your women in agreement to this and what about the Grand Council?"

"Well Paul, as you know, when your woman talks, you listen and ours have told us to get a set of balls, swallow our pride and ask for help," the Samson Chief said and everyone in the room laughed.

"As well you should," Emily said. "Why Paul would make no decisions at all if were not for me."

Paul could only shake his head as he was now the brunt of the jokes.

"As far as the Grand Council," the Chief continued. "They have no say in how we run our bands or Reserves."

"We ask ourselves," the Ermineskin Chief said. "Why is it that we have more natural resource money than you do, less people and yet have so little to show for it? The Indian Affairs man showed us his history of your people and he was right. Your people lived on the land and were warriors like us. Your system of government and how your Host is set up is similar to ours. Why then are things so different? We asked this of our selves many times and the only answer we could come up with was that you were white and we were not."

Paul sighed and after a moment to gather his thoughts said, "And that my friend is your biggest problem. It is always because of discrimination. We came to this country and most of us could not speak the language. Most of us were Catholics and very few were English or French. Believe me, to this day we have our share of discrimination. We, like you, have kept our traditions and among ourselves, speak our cultural languages. Unlike you, we do not let those differences get in the way of our dealings with the outside world. Like it or not, we are a part of Canada and have to function within that society. This you have resisted."

"Yes we are beginning to understand that," the Samson Chief said. "It has taken our young people and their access to the internet to make us aware of the bigger world."

"In the beginning, our people were like yours," Paul said. "We were strangers in a strange land with different customs and language. Unlike in this country, that other land stole from us and killed us. But the leaders in that country did the same to everyone, not just us. We worked hard and gained the trust of the local people and they accepted us. In fact, many of them joined us here when we came to Canada and many came after, when the Bolsheviks made life intolerable for them. We have united as a group and together we have made this a land of plenty and abundance for ourselves and our descendants."

"This too is what we crave," the oldest of the group said. "To get out of the cycle of poverty, sickness and death."

Paul sighed. "To be like us, you must do what we do. Even then it may not work."

"But we have tried," the elder said. "We have invested large sums of money in businesses and failed time and time again. We have tried to set up hospitals and schools with the governments help, but we fail again. Everything we try fails and still we have nothing."

"Bullshit!" Elizabeth said smashing her fist onto the table. "You still have each other. The faith you have in one another, the hope for a better life. That is not nothing. When my husband was killed, I was not thinking of his unborn son or his family or my family. All I was thinking about was my pain and how I wanted it to end. It took a young woman, a woman I didn't even know, to pick me up and make me feel as if I really belonged. As if my life still had meaning. There is always hope, unless you quit trying."

Emily stood and held her now crying daughter for a moment.

"I'm sorry," Elizabeth said. "I haven't thought about that day for a very long time. Please forgive my outburst."

"All right then," Emily said. "Let's address the elephant in the room, no more bullshit. There are several big differences between your people and ours and race is only a small part of it. Unlike you, we do not depend on the government for anything. In fact it is often the opposite and believe me when I tell you, we make the government pay every time we help them. Next, we embrace our culture, our whole culture, not just the touchy, touchy feel good things. We also embrace the bad, the times we were down, when we had nothing, when we were starving or left to die on our own in some God forsaken part of the world, far from home and family. As a culture, you must be willing to do this. Yes, the Whiteman and the government has at times treated you badly and you have gotten bad advice from well-meaning people, but at the end of the day it is your responsibility as leaders to ensure that never happens again."

"That is only the beginning and is an ongoing thing, not just for we the leaders, but for everyone," Paul said. "Our schools and university and hospitals, we built our selves. The same with our roads, sewer and water systems. Our people build them, run them, staff them and maintain them. We pay for those things by taxing our people and businesses a flat ten percent tax. We also pay the federal Government ten percent of all the Earldoms revenues. We are not required to, but we feel that we have to. In addition, it is mandatory for each person and business to contribute ten percent of their earnings to a charity of their choice."

"Yes," the Samson chief said. "This we would also like, but we lack the expertise."

"We can help you with that," Elizabeth said. "But only for a short time. Then you will have to take responsibility yourselves."

"One difference we have in our charter that you do not in your treaty is this," Emily said. "We are required to field a fully trained and equipped battalion from each Earldom in times of national emergency, time of war, or at the request of Her Majesty directly. As a result, at the beginning of July on the year each citizen reaches their eighteenth birthday and finishes their Grade Twelve or GED, it is mandatory that they serve a minimum of five years in our regiments. If they choose not to, they become a citizen of Canada at large and are expected to pay all taxes and other requirements of any other Canadian Citizen. They are not banned from the colony, but are not allowed the privileges of it."

"How many people are in a battalion?" the Ermineskin chief asked.

"Our battalions consist of one thousand officers and enlisted personnel in the combat specialty and one thousand officers and enlisted personnel in the support specialty," Elizabeth said.

"But we only graduate twenty five students most years," the eldest elder said. "We could never get that high a number."

"We could easily integrate your people with ours," Emily said. "It would not stretch our training people to far. I also think that very quickly, you would see your dropout rates fall from eighty percent, to less than twenty in a very short period of time. I would recommend that you offer the program to anyone below the age of thirty as well."

"But still we would be far short of a battalion," the Elder said. "We could not field a full battalion as you do."

"You could integrate with us or one of the regular Canadian Forces battalions," Elizabeth said.

"I don't know how such things happen," the Elder said. "But I think we would rather be with you if it can be arranged."

"Elizabeth," Paul said. "How busy is the cadet commander and can he handle setting up a new group?"

"The staff are all good," Elizabeth said. "I think he is rather bored and would like the challenge."

Paul stood, walked to the door opened it and beckoned his aide forward.

"Ask the cadet commander to join us at his earliest convenience," Paul said. "Also, have some one in records make two copies of our colony bylaws and minimum military standards. Then see what the Warrant has in way of lunch for us and have all that brought to us if you please."

"Yes sir. The Federal people are asking how things are going sir."

"Negotiations are proceeding and making progress," Paul said. "Ask them if there is anything we can do for them. Possibly a tour of the base? The Cadet training facility? Have the Cadet staff available and tell them to answer any questions and to be cooperative as much as possible."

By the time Paul had re-entered the room and closed the door, his aide had delegated tasks to the other aides and they were scurrying out the mess hall door to make things happen.

"I have taken the liberty to have some copies of our colony bylaws and minimum regimental standards sent over," he said siting down once again. "I have also asked our Cadet Commander to join us. If he meets your standards and is in agreement, I will ask him to set up and run your Cadet program for you until you have qualified people to take over. The military is very much a top down organization I am afraid. Your Cadets would be under our control and we report to the Canadian Cadets, who are in turn under the control of DND. As is the Regiment itself, as long as it is within the scope of our commitment agreement that is. Shit!"

"Major!" Paul called out and the door was quickly opened. "I am going to need two copies of our military agreement with the Canadian Government as well."

"I took the liberty of doing that already sir," his aide said.

"Ok good. Give yourself a cookie," Paul said, as the Major shut the door again.

"Em, see if you can find him a good job please," Paul said. "He is ready for command."

"Sure," Emily said. "It's way past time. I have asked him before, but he keeps refusing."

"If he refuses again, tell him to see me," Paul said.

"Gentlemen, I recommend that you read over the material I will give to you. Discuss it with your councils, tweak it to suit your needs and if you wish, we can then have an agreement set up with ourselves and possibly the Feds. What do you think?"

The six men looked at each other and quickly agreed.

"Emily? Countess?" Paul asked his wife and daughter, who both nodded their heads in agreement.

Paul stood and extended his hand to the eldest of the Elders.

"Well then gentlemen, I think you have an agreement with the Earldoms of Didsbury and Olds."

All the people in the room stood and shook hands with each other sealing the deal.

"I wonder," the elder said. "Would it be possible for you to help us with some of our contracts and civil dealings? You seem to make out better than we do in yours."

"It is within our charter and is an obligation to render civil assistance to any Alberta First Nations organization that asks us for it," Emily said. "We have our own accountants and lawyers. If you wish, I can have them contact your people and have them go over your books and contracts."

"How long has that been in place?" the Ermineskin chief asked. "It's the first I have heard of it."

"Our founder insisted on it when we first received our charter," Emily said. "We were the only organized government in the area at the time and he wanted to ensure we could help without waiting for Federal approval. Indian Affairs may or may not be aware of it and would probably not want you to know about it in any case."

"And should we wish to start an endeavour," the Sampson chief said. "You would help us too?"

"If you asked," Paul said. "And if it met with our standards, we would most likely help you with the start up. We do that all of the time among ourselves. We generally require a full seat on the board and twenty percent of the company."

The room went silent for a while.

"These are better terms that what we get now," the Sampson chief said. "It is us who gets the twenty percent, usually less."

"Yes well, we take a more long term approach on things than most companies do," Paul said. "But, I think you will find we are very picky on what we fund. If we can't make a profit, we won't fund it."

"On behalf of the Sampson First Nations, I ask for your assistance."

"I too, on behalf of the ErmineSkin First Nations."

"On behalf of the Bekenbaum Family Trust, I agree to provide assistance on deserving projects," Paul said.

Once again, the group rose and shook hands. Paul explained to them that sometimes the Andreas Host would be funding projects and sometimes the family trust and sometimes they might receive help from other individual family or host members or businesses depending on the risk level. A knock and the door opening, quieted the room and they all sat down as a large man in full uniform, his beret tucked under his left arm, marched into the room and crashed to attention in front of Paul.

"Sir! You requested my presence sir!" the man said.

"At Ease Major," Paul growled and the Major assumed parade rest, his eyes focused two inches above Paul's head.

From the top of his jet black hair, to the tips of his gleaming jump boots, the major was impeccable. He stood six foot six and weighed over two hundred well fit pounds. The black hair, prominent cheek bones and amber tinged skin, betrayed his heritage. On his right uniform sleeve, above the cuff, were five gold rings, denoting five years of service each. The Eagle and crossed Winchester rifles on his collar points gleamed in the light given off from the florescent fixtures of the room. Above both breast pockets were rows of qualification and awards ribbons and he stood head held high and shoulders squared. The epitome of self-confidence.

"This gentlemen, is Major Albert Whitefeather. He is the commander of our Cadet Corps," Elizabeth said. "As you can see from his 'I was there' ribbons, he has been there and done that. We are lucky to have him. He has won almost every decoration there is to be won in the Canadian Army. He has decorations from all of the NATO countries and several other countries. At his insistence, he is the Cadet Corps Commander. We had other plans for him."

"At the age of thirteen," Paul said. "Albert fell in with a group on his reserve that called themselves the Cheyanne Brotherhood. By the age of sixteen, he was one of their leaders. What they were doing, makes your kids goings on seem like child's play. His grandmother called her cousin, a member of our host, worried about Albert's future. He was sent up here and has been here ever since."

"Big Indian," Elizabeth said. "These Elders have asked us for help. We thought a Cadet program would be beneficial. What do you think?"

"Countess," Albert said. "The Major agrees. The Major believes it will instil discipline, loyalty and self-respect in the Cadets Mam."

"A Cheyanne teaching a bunch of Cree Kids?" the eldest elder blurted out.

"Something wrong with that?" Paul asked. "The Cree feel they cannot lower themselves to the Cheyanne level? The Major's great-grandfather fought alongside my Great-grandfather. I can vouch for the Major personally. He is one of the finest men I have had the privilege to know."

"Big Indian sit down," Emily said. "You're making my neck sore."

"Ya well, maybe if you worked out more, that lovely neck would be in better shape," Albert said. "How fresh is that coffee?"

"What you doing after work sweetie?" Albert asked Emily. "I've got a nice new ride I could show you."

"And your wife and kids would have my ass for it you big dummy," Emily said.

"What's all this about then?" Albert asked. "You want me to set up a Cadet Corp for these people? DND will approve?"

"If they don't, we'll just make their program a chapter of ours and bypass it," Paul said.

Albert said nothing and just sat looking at the six elders across from him as he sipped his coffee. They began to get a little uncomfortable from the silence and the watching eyes of the four veteran soldiers across from them who sat drinking their coffee quietly.

"I think," the Ermineskin chief said. "That I speak for the Samson band in this and for my band, that it would be an honour for us to have a member of the Cheyanne Nation head our Cadet Corps. Would it be possible for the Major to set that up for us?"

Albert said nothing, waiting for one of the other officers to respond, which they did not and he finally got the hint.

"Gentlemen, it would be an honour for this humble servant to assist you in this matter," Albert said. "With the General's and the Colonels permission, I would like to personally take charge of this mission."

"Do we agree on this matter then?" Paul asked.

Once again, including Albert this time, all the people in the room stood and shook hands. Paul hollered for the major and ordered a bottle of vodka and a round of beers for everyone.

Paul himself poured the glasses of vodka after he had banished his aide once again and raised his glass.

"To our new partnership and our new brothers," he said, then drained the glass as did the others.

"Damn that's good shit," the eldest elder said. This time he poured all the glasses full and raised his glass.

"To a brighter future for our children," he said. And once again the glasses were emptied.

"Woa, good shit," he said once again. "Alright enough of that or I'll be falling down stupid in five minutes."

"Shit, you're falling down stupid when you're sober John," Paul said.

"You been talking with my wife again ain't you," John said and the room laughed.

After three rounds of beer, the conference room was becoming chummy. All of the people in it, except for Albert, had met each other in the past and in the case of Paul and John, were old friends. Albert started telling war stories from his younger days and at one point spoke of a story that involved Paul and Emily in their younger days that Elizabeth had not even heard. The story was wild and loud, each participant ending it with yells.

A concerned Indian Affairs man rushed up to Paul's aid.

"There is something wrong. They are arguing in there!" he said.

"Nothing to be concerned about I assure you sir," the Major said, who had also never heard that particular story.

"Well you should go in and see," the man said. "I am concerned."

The major opened and went through the door, closing it behind him.

"General," he said. "Indian Affairs is becoming concerned about the tone of the negotiations sir and wonders if he could perhaps intervene and calm things down."

"Shit if things were anymore calmer, we'd be sleeping," Albert said.

"Major," Paul said. "Tell Indian Affairs we are just tidying up a final point and will be with them very shortly and give the Junior Ranks Club a heads up that the guests will be leaving shortly."

The now eleven people in the conference room, re-entered the Officers Mess, jackets and ties back in position and solemnly sat at their respective tables. Not a hint of what had transpired on their faces. Paul nodded at the Warrant Officer who had a quick word in the back and several bottles of vodka appeared and glasses were poured and placed in front of each person at the respective tables. The servers stood behind the tables, bottles in hand.

"It is my pleasure," Paul said. "To announce, that after some very hard negotiations, the Samson and Ermineskin First Nations have come to an agreement in principle with the Andreas Host as far as the Cadet training Corp and several other minor points that need not concern Indian Affairs, has been achieved. Of course, this agreement in principle must be studied and approved by all three bands before it can be signed. Indian Affairs and DND will be informed when it is. Can we be assured that we will have Indian Affairs and DND approval?"

"I have been told," Indian Affairs said. "By the Minister himself, that the Prime Minister had told him we had better approve of whatever the people in Didsbury said, or they would go to a higher authority to get what they want."

"Very well then," Paul said. "It is the custom of my people to toast the accomplishment of an agreement. To the future of our peoples!"

The glasses were quickly refilled.

"To the continued cooperation among our peoples," the Eldest Elder said.

Indian Affairs rose, "To Canada."

"To her Majesty," the RCMP Inspector said.

"Ok, enough already," Paul said. "Now, before the lawyers and bureaucrats get involved, the PM was right. Her Majesty will take a deep personal interest in this matter. The First Nations and the Major have agreed on the Cadet Corp question, it is up to you to fast track acceptance. As far as we are concerned, we have an agreement and will proceed as such. Now it has been a long and hard day and I am sure you would all like to get back to your families."

After a round of final handshakes, all but the RCMP Inspector and his people, left the building and cars were heard starting up and leaving.

Paul waved his hand over his head and loosening his tie and unbuttoning his tunic, sat down.

"Major, thank you for your service and all the other aides as well today. Steak and beer on me tonight gentlemen, ladies," Paul said raising his beer in salute to the aides who had spent all day running errands and fielding questions.

"Jesus," the Inspector said. "I thought sure the deal was off right at the end there with all the yelling."

"That?" Paul said. "That was John telling us a story about he and my father back in the old days playing hockey against each other. We had all the negotiations done within an hour and five minutes after Big

Indian joined us, we finalized it. This last bit was just theatre to make it look like it was a hard fought deal on both sides."

"So who's idea was this anyway?" the Inspector asked.

"Kind of a mutual deal," Paul said. "John called and asked us what they should do. They had tried everything and I suggested this. Then they took over from there."

"So you were playing us?"

"No, not really," Paul said. "They are more familiar with their politics than I am, but we have more experience and expertise dealing with government BS than they do. So we just cooperated. I think within a generation those two bands will be the envy of the First Nations."

"You might as well stay over Liz," Paul said as the three Bekenbaums walked home from the base. "No sense waking up the little gaffer just to try and put him to sleep after."

"No argument there Pop," Elizabeth said. "Between the booze and the long day, I've about had it."

"I suppose there is no way Gadgets Gang, will be home for Christmas then?" Emily asked.

"They have set up surveillance and a good target in Tora Bora," Paul said. "I think they have done enough and I am going to pull them out. No guarantees, but if they all survive, they should be home within the week."

"God grant it so," Emily said.

"From your lips to His ears," Elizabeth said and the group finished the walk in silence.

Chapter Five

"Alright," Rick said, plunking himself down at the makeshift table in front of Bashir. "I don't need Regiment confirmation on the high value of these targets. There are several of Americas most wanted in that group. There appears to be only thirty of them on site at this time so we should hit them hard and fast. Julia is going to send the intel anyway, but we should hit them tomorrow and I have a new idea to put to you."

"Go ahead my friend," Bashir said. "I have learned to value your judgment."

"The Major tells me you have met all of these people and worked with some of them in the past?" Paul asked.

"Yes against the Russians, we worked with many of these people," Bashir said. "We do not agree with their politics, but we worked with them for a common goal."

"So I propose to use that familiarity against them. That you ride in tomorrow and make buddy buddy, surround them casually, give my people and I a signal and we take out the guards while you take the rest prisoner. What do you think?"

Bashir looked at his Major and gestured him to speak.

"It is as he says," Akmed said. "There are many high ranking people there. Also, the only ones armed are the guards and the two machine gun crews. We can easily take control of the rest after they are dealt with."

"This sounds like it is what we should do," Bashir said. "How will I give the signal?"

"I will give you a head set that you can put under your turban," Rick said. "When all is ready, just give us the word and we start shooting."

"Good, we go first thing and should be there just after morning prayers," Bashir said.

"Good. Now one final detail before Julia makes her transmission," Rick said. "I need your permission to set up two bank accounts. One for your tribe and one for your troopers."

"Why would we need these?" Bashir said.

"So far, while you have been with us," Rick said. "We have collected three million US dollars in bounties. It will be somewhat more after tomorrow, but I can't tell you how much at this time. It is our custom to split the money. In this case, one third to my Regiment, one third to yours and one third to be split among the troops involved."

"What!"Akmed blurted out. "Why, we are all rich! Even the lowliest private."

Bashir was dumbfounded and at a loss for words.

"Me, I have my eye on a nice Mercedes and I see a nice long trip somewhere where the sun is nice and the females nicer," Rick said. "If I make it out of here."

"One million dollars Akmed. We can build a hospital and send our children to Britain for schooling. We can buy some tractors and combines."

"And maybe I can buy some better horses to beat your ass," Akmed said.

"The Americans would do this?" Bashir said.

"My father will insist on it, you can be assured and the Americans have learned not to play us false," Rick said. "It generally costs them double if they do."

"You would do this for us?" Bashir said.

"Why not?" Rick said. "You were just as much responsible for the results as we were. You deserve it. You won't get a share of the first raid though. That's all our baby."

"Oh, no problem," Bashir said. "It is only fitting. My God, thank you, you have no idea what you have just done for my people."

"Don't thank me yet," Rick said. "One more raid to finish. It is more important that we train and plan well than to count money we do not have yet. Our people's lives depend on it."

The regiment was in place before dawn and Rick had the sites of his custom made Barrette fifty caliber sniper rifle on his designated target as Bashir's band rode into the Al-Qaida camp. The last supply drop had included their own sniper rifles and Rick and the two snipers had their own familiar weapons at last. The Russian rifles had been given to other shooters as had the Afghan sniper rifles. Each shooter had a designated target to take out, Ricks was a heavy machine gun crew about six hundred yards away. An easy distance for this rifle.

Bashir and his group were welcomed as old comrades into the camp and Rick carefully counted as more came out of the caves and joined the celebration. He noticed that Bashir's people made sure they were blocking the entrance to the cave system and that they all kept their weapons with them and were slowly ringing the targets.

"Standby," Rick said into his mike, as he saw Bashir take a look around while listening to a man. Bashir casually pull the microphone down from under his turban.

"Eagles claw and Bears maul," came Bashir's voice over Ricks head set.

Rick sited on the gunner and touched the trigger. "Five, four, three, two, one," he said into his mike and gently squeezed the trigger after one. The rifle in his hands roared and he shifted target to the assistant gunner and had him sited and was squeezing the trigger as the first round hit the gunner and threw him backwards. As the assistant turned his head to see what had happened to his comrade, his bullet smashed into his chest, throwing him backward as well.

"Good hit primary," Julia said. "Good hit secondary." She took her eyes from her spotting scope and looked for other targets. Rick doing the same with his rifle scope.

All the spotters for the other snipers reported in with good target hits. Now the Canadians scanned the surprised group below for any more possible targets or need for assistance. Bashir's people had things well in hand and the enemy were all on their knees with hands locked behind heads and were being roughly kicked down so they were lying face down on the ground and being covered by troopers holding AKs at their heads. Other troopers were walking among them with plastic zip ties. Tying arms behind backs and legs together then forcing the legs up and zip tying them to the hands.

"Target secure," Bashir said into the radio. "All enemy accounted for."

"Roger," Rick said. "All Charley, converge on the camp. Keep on the lookout for strays."

Rick and the rest of the commando rose like phantoms from their places of concealment and causally, with weapons at the ready and scanning continually, made their way down into the cave complex. Only once they reached the area and guards were placed on the perimeter did the celebration begin, with much cheering and firing of weapons into the air.

"My God," Bashir said. "Even with knowing what we were doing, the sudden violence and noise scared even me. It was like the hand of God plucked those men from their positions. Almost at the same time, those men flew backward, then we heard the guns."

"It is always better to give, than to receive," Bill said with a smile on his face.

"Fucking Russians," one of the men lying in the dirt said and spat.

"In your dreams asshole," Julia said. "A fucking Russian would be shitting his pants in terror if he saw us."

"Ok people, we don't have time for this now." Rick said. "I need pictures of all these guys and the ones we killed. I hope none of you took head shots, it might cost you a lot of money. I want all these guys stripped of anything in their pockets. I need these caves cleared out and any info brought to Julia ASAP. We need all this done before we lose sat comms or the Yanks get wind of it."

The place was soon buzzing with activity. Rick, Bill and Patricia helped Julia with the data collection as there was to much for her to handle by herself. It was very quickly determined that there was no way they had enough storage capability for all of the computer files they found. Julia began the lengthy transmission and Rick knew that it would be to long a transmission for the Americans to not detect.

"Bashir, I think it wise that you get your people out of here," Rick said. "I am going to have to ask for help with all this and I don't think it wise for the CIA or MI6 to find out you were helping us."

"I agree," Bashir said. "I see how they are hounding you people. We do not need that aggravation." He barked out a series of orders and his people jumped into motion, grabbing whatever cash and valuables they had discovered and weapons and ammunition. Rick had his people give back the rifles they had borrowed, as well as their own Russian sniper weapons and the light machine guns along with most of their spare ammunition, keeping only the loaded clips they had.

Bashir came to Rick and gave him a big hug, kissing him on both cheeks, tears in his eyes.

"Once again your people have helped us and once again we are in your debt," he said. "One day soon, I hope to repay all you have done for us."

Many bonds had been made between the two groups over the past three months and there were not many dry eyes among either group as the Afghans rode off, all the horses with them, leaving the Canadians behind, alone.

"Give them an hour," Rick said to Julia. "Then start sending the data. I wonder what he meant by once again you have helped us. Do you know something I don't?"

"Nope, it's a mystery to me too," she said.

An hour later, as Julia started to up load all the data home via satellite, Rick, for the first time in three months tuned his radio to the command net.

"Alpha Whiskey, Alpha Whiskey, this is Echo Charley over," he said.

Hearing nothing, he started again after checking with Julia if he was broadcasting.

"Alpha Whiskey, Alpha Whiskey, this is Echo Charley over."

"Station calling Alpha Whiskey say again," came the response.

"Alpha Whiskey, this is Echo Charley, read you six by eight over."

"Echo Charley, Alpha Whiskey, nine by nine. Wait one."

"Echo Charley, this is Alpha Six Actual," came a different voice. *"Let me talk with your commander."*

"Alpha Six Actual this is Charley One over," Rick said.

"Where the hell have you people been Charley One? We have been trying to locate you for three months!"

"Sorry sir. We got lost and had to be rescued by some locals and were under orders to keep radio silence."

"Highly unprofessional Charley One. Your superiors will be notified of our displeasure."

"Roger Alpha Six. We could use some assistance at our location sir."

"Typical, ask the Americans for help when your balls are in a jam. Go ahead with your request."

"We have thirty high profile prisoners, eight enemy dead, a bunch of documents and computers full of data. We are almost out of rations and our boots and ammo are running thin."

"You've got what?"

"Thirty high ranking Al-Qaida prisoners, eight dead and to many documents for us to handle sir."

"I heard you the first time. We have your coordinates. Three Chinooks will be at your location within the hour. Stay put."

"Roger Alpha Six Actual. Ah, can we be extracted with the prisoners sir. A warm shower, clean clothing and good food, would be nice sir."

"Yes, yes of course. Just hang in there Charley One. We are on our way."

It wasn't three Chinooks that arrived and hour and a half later, but five. A number of fighter planes could be seen circling overhead as the big twin rotor aircraft thundered into view. The first two landed, rear ramps already opened. Fully armed and armoured troops poured, out securing the perimeter, as the other three landed and more troops came out. The Canadians came down from their positions as all this was going on, shouldered weapons and for the first time in a long time, smiled and relaxed.

Troopers began converging on the prisoners, wire cutters in hand, cut the leg tethers and hustled them into the waiting helicopters. A group of officers, pristine desert camouflaged uniforms, helmets and body armour approached the lounging Canadians, who slowly stood and saluted as they approached.

"Which one of you is Charley One?" the general leading the group asked, looking in vain for any rank markings on the Canadians.

"Warrant Smith sir," Rick said.

"Ya and I am General Wesson, sure," the General said. "I bet you are all Smith and Wesson's."

"That would be correct sir," Rick said. "How may I help the general sir?"

"Well, before CIA gets here, I just wanted to say well done. I don't know what they put in the water where you people come from, but you should bottle it and sell it. You ten people did more by yourselves than the rest of my Special Forces people did all together. With your help, we have dealt al-Qaida a severe blow. Colonel, I believe you owe these people an apology."

"Yes sir," a colonel said. "I apologize for my behaviour on the radio Warrant Smith."

"No problem sir, I would have been pissed too," Rick said. "Unfortunately I was following our ROE's and SOPs sir."

"Well our people should take lessons from you people," the Colonel said. "There are only ten of you?"

"We had some local help sir," Rick said. "They choose not to be recognized for it sir."

"Can't say as I blame them," the general said. "That's a good idea though. Maybe we should send some of our people to train with yours."

"Didn't seem to help sir," Bill said. "I trained that SEAL group that was looking for us."

"Oh shit, I should have known," the general said. "Trust the Canadians to send their best people and not let us know about it."

"I am afraid we are far from the best general," Rick said. "We were just the ones that were handy at the time."

"Well you get your butts on my helicopter. You have done enough. Major go with them and make sure they get the best when they get back to camp and put it on my tab. Now git. Those are CIA in that chopper that is arriving now. They'll have you here for days."

"What I could do with a battalion of those people," the colonel said, as the ten commandos shouldered their worn packs and headed for the Chinook.

"Four thousand of them kicked some serious Iraqi ass during Desert Storm," the general said. "The Saudis got the credit for it, but it was those guys who did all the work."

"Christ that was those guys?" the colonel exclaimed. "I'm glad they are on our side."

"Warrant Smith," the major asked after the helicopter had reached altitude. "What would you like to do first when we land?"

"The thickest steaks you can find and a cold six pack of beer, for each of us, sir," Rick said loudly and was greeted by hurrahs by all the rest of the commando. "Then a shower, fresh uniforms and a good bed would be nice."

"No problem," the major said. "A battalion of PPCLI has just arrived, I can arrange accommodation with them after you chow down with us."

"That won't be necessary major," Rick said. "After chow, our own people will be picking us up."

Looking out the window as they came into the base, Rick could see that a rather large group of people had gathered around the landing pad. Many of them international press people. Rick pointed at the window and dug out his balaclava from his pack and donned it, adjusting it so that it covered his face from his nose downward. The rest of the commando followed suit and to the disappointment of the gathered press, no questions were answered or requests for interviews acknowledged as they made their way out of the Chinook and toward the waiting truck.

Once out of view of the members of the press, the balaclavas came off again, but they still made a stir as they entered the mess hall, AKs on one shoulder and packs on the other. Weapons belts full of clips and grenades still on. Their dusty, dirty and well-worn uniforms in stark contrast to the crisp clean uniforms of the rest of the mess hall occupants. A hush came over the mess hall as the Canadians made their way to a table set aside for them and they sat, dumping their packs at their feet and resting the loaded AKs against the table. Servers were waiting and placed plates of steak with all the trimming in front of each trooper, while others put a tall bottle of beer. Rick sat and stared at them for a minute, before taking hold of the beer, waving it at his troopers and guzzling it back, not stopping until it was finished. The rest of the gang followed suit.

"God damn, I missed that!" Rick said. "Even if it's Yankee piss beer."

As they were almost finished wolfing down their dinners, a group of soldiers approached, uniforms starched and aviator glasses perched on noses. A blond officer in an impeccable green camouflage uniform was with them. "These are the troopers I was speaking of Major," The SEAL commander said in Russian.

"Mon due!" Al exclaimed in French. "Cheri, where have you been all my life."

"These are not my people," Rick heard a female voice say behind them in Ukrainian.

He spun around with a witty comeback ready. It died in his throat as he beheld the most striking green eyes he had ever seen, framed by blond, almost white hair. The rest of the package was just as striking and she began to turn crimson as the male members of the commando feasted on her beauty, but most especially Rick who was right in front of her.

"You have wasted my time here," she said angrily.

"But mam, they told us they were Ukrainian," the SEAL said.

Rick stood awkwardly, trying in vain to gather his thoughts. "Oh shit, the mighty Gadget has finally been silenced," Julia said in German. "And by a wee woman no less."

"Just who the hell are you people anyway!" the SEAL demanded.

"I apologize for the confusion Major," Rick said in Ukrainian. "The commander asked us where we were from originally and I told him Ukraine, which is not really lying, my ancestors were from there. The Commander never was very observant, even when he was training with us."

Rick pointed to the Canada patch on his shoulder. "Would the Major care to join us? I am afraid they only serve substandard beer and the vodka is probably just as bad, but you are welcome in any case to join us."

"I have been humiliated enough thank you!" she said and stalked off.

"Oh my," Rick said. "If she is anything like my great grandmother was, you are in a heap of shit Commander."

The SEALS took off chasing the angry Ukrainian officer to the laughs of the commando and most of the mess hall. It wasn't often the SEALs were shown up.

"Not to worry Rick," Julia said. "I'll find out who she is and you can apologize again."

"Ya that would be nice," Rick said quietly. "Unfortunately it will have to be from long distance. We are going home."

"What! When!" now Rick had the complete attention of the whole commando.

"The pilots are standing by the door," Rick said pointing. "Unless you want to have a shower and a sleep first."

"Shit no!" Al yelled. "I can do that at home! Get me out of here!"

Sixteen hours later they landed and were sleeping that night in their own beds.

Chapter Six

It was starting to get warm under the lights of the stage and Rick was fighting hard to stay awake. He was still, after a month, getting used to the time change and getting up early to make sure his dress uniform was perfect had not helped any. The ten commandos were sitting in a row to one side of the stage and so far had endured all the speeches and the individual presentations to each graduate of this year's class. This year had seen the inclusion of three Ukrainian troopers. Ukraine was pushing to be included in NATO and had joined with seven Polish troopers to make up the full complement of ten. Al mumbled an apology under his breath as he shifted uncomfortable in his chair and jangled Rick's uncomfortable and unfamiliar sword. It was only on very rare occasions that full dress uniform with all the medals and accruements was required and graduation ceremonies was one of them. It was at times like this, when Rick fully appreciated what his family had accomplished, because now, in all their finery and with full medals on display instead of the tiny bits of cloth, that he could see just how much they had accomplished. He was amazed his father could even stand with all the metal on his chest and his mother's as well. After casually gazing at the crowd in the auditorium, his roving eyes fell on the regimental colours and all of battle streamers on it and he realized how proud he was of that flag and all it represented. He had missed his father rising and striding to the microphone at the front of the podium.

"First Commando front and centre!" his father commanded.

With a clash and rattle of swords and a final stomp of boots, the ten commandos arranged themselves in the centre of the stage, facing the crowd and behind the general.

"Honoured guests, ladies and gentlemen, parents and graduates," Paul said. "It is not often that we have the honour of combining a graduation ceremony with the reception of our heroes back to our home. This is one of them. Six years ago, this group of young people behind me were sitting in those same chairs you graduates are sitting in right now. They have just returned from three months of duty fighting our enemies in Afghanistan. Three months of continual duty, behind the lines in enemy held territory. Along with our Afghan Allies, they were responsible for the destruction of over three hundred al-Qaida and Taliban fighters and terrorists. The capture of thirty high ranking al-Qaida officials and the killing of three internationally wanted terror bombers. They have captured thousands of pages of enemy documents. Documents that outlined future terror plots and the names of hundreds of other terrorists. And in the words of Her Majesty, 'You have been responsible for the saving of untold thousands of civilians.' Her Majesty mentions each one of these troopers individually, by name and deed in her dispatch. For those of you unfamiliar with our military, to be named in any dispatch is an honour, but to be named in a Royal dispatch is one of the highest honours a common trooper can receive."

"These young troopers deserve our respect and admiration. They have done our Sovereign, our country, our regiment and their families proud. Commando One, I salute you."

Paul turned around and came to attention.

"Regiment, Attention!" Elizabeth called out. Everyone in uniform in the auditorium rose and came to attention. "Regiment, Salute!" As one, the regiment and every other person wearing a uniform in the crowd saluted.

"Graduates," Paul continued after everyone but the commando had resumed their seats. "This is the standard that we expect from each and every one of you. Not all of you will have the opportunity to make as much of an impact as Commando One has, but we expect each and every one of you to do your best at what ever task you are sent to accomplish. Our ancestors and our traditions demand it. I demand it. Your country demands it and your family and friends demand it!"

"Graduates Attention!" he commanded. "Graduates dismissed, fall out and where's the damn booze."

Rick was leaning against the wall, the top button of his dress uniform undone and his tie loose. He had a bottle of beer in his right hand and was looking over Al's head scanning the crowd of people, young and old on the dance floor half listening to Al and his latest story. It was almost time for him to quietly disappear, Rick was never much of a party goer, preferring the quiet intimate parties to the large noisy ones.

"Oh lala," Al said. "Mon Cheri, once again you grace us with your vision of beauty. It can only mean you have fallen under the spell of I, the Great Al."

Rick was not even going to look around at the latest of Al's many infatuations, when a sweet Ukrainian accented English began to speak.

"Well I was just wondering if the Master Warrant was not to busy, if he would honour me with a dance so that he might apologize in person."

Rick spun around so fast he almost tripped. There before him, in her best uniform, was the cute Ukrainian Major that had captivated him back in Kabul.

"Um, yes mam, sure mam, anything you say mam," he stumbled out.

Julia pushed him forward so that he stumbled against the Major. "Shit," she said. "The bloody man turns to mush at the first sight of some cute blond. Come on Al, I'm tired of standing here watching everyone else having fun. You're dancing with me."

"Once again, the female is helplessly under the spell of the mighty Al," he said.

"In your dreams lover boy," Julia said and dragged him away, leaving Rick and the Major alone.

"After you mam," Rick said, gesturing to the dance floor.

An old time slow waltz started to play and he took her into his arms. His heart started to race as he took in the smell of her hair and her perfume. She moved gracefully and lightly on her feet and he almost missed her words as she began to speak. When he looked down at her into her bright green eyes his heart skipped a beat.

"I said Master Warrant," she said. "Has the cat got your tongue? Or is my accent so bad you cannot understand me?"

"No mam, you are beautiful mam," Rick stammered. "Oh shit, I mean you speak English beautifully mam." Christ I'm blowing this big time, he thought.

"Well Master Warrant, this is a social occasion, you and I are both officers and this mam nonsense is rather tedious. I am Tanya Helenchuk and you are?"

"Richard Bekenbaum mam. Shit sorry Ms. Helenchuk I mean."

"It is Miss not Ms and Tanya, Richard," she said with a grin. "Now I am still waiting for that apology." Her eyes were twinkling in the lights and Rick had trouble focusing on anything else.

"Look Tanya, if I caused you any discomfort it was unintentional," Rick said. "Those damn SEALS came waltzing in like big shots and I couldn't help but show them up. And my ancestors really did come here from Ukraine."

"Apology accepted Richard and I too would like to apologize for my behaviour that day," she said. "I was not upset with you, but that stupid Navy Commander who dragged me down there and made me waste my day. Well not really waste. I did get to meet you after all. Yes I know this, that your family comes from Ukraine. In fact from the same district as mine. Your family is quiet famous there."

"Well then you know more than I do," Rick said. "I'm just a minor farmer in a small community of farmers, who just happens to be in the army."

"Yes, I too am the same," Tanya said. "Just a small farm girl who happens to be in the army."

"Look, if you would prefer, it is just as easy for me to speak in your language," Rick said in Russian.

"No, no," Tanya said in English. "If you don't mind, I don't get much chance to use my English and it is a big part of my job now. Were you guys really behind the lines for three months with no support?"

"Pretty much. We were with thirty or so Afghans, good people and we were in regular contact back here. When we needed it, we were air supplied. We got our ammo mostly from captured supplies, which is why we were using Russian equipment instead of our own."

"My three troopers have nothing but good things to say about their training here," Tanya said. "They are three of our best and they said your kids made them look sick."

"Well we are Cossacks you know, would you expect anything different from us?"

"You have kept your traditions?" she asked.

Just then the music changed to a slow Russian beat.

"Pretty much," Rick said.

"Then you would know what this song means and the dance moves?"

The dance floor was emptying out and Tanya moved to the centre and putting her head high and her arms wide, began to dance in a circle around Rick as he stood and admired the finely shaped legs that were showing beneath what he realized was a shorter than normal uniforms skirt. She frowned at him as he just stood there and he realized she expected him to join her. He put one hand on a hip, raised his head high and with an exaggerated leg movement, spun away so his back was to her, forcing her to dance to his front. Now she had a puzzled look on her face as he once again raised his head and spun his back toward her.

Once again she was forced to dance in front of him. She was not used to this behaviour, it was usually her turning away from the men. Suddenly, there were three other girls on the dance floor vying for Rick's attention, one striking girl actually touching him, running her hand down his arm. Tanya was not used to this much competition and she found herself warming to the challenge. Stomping her foot on the ground demanding his attention, as she began her intricate moves. A crowd had formed a circle around them and begun to sing the song that went with the music, slowly clapping hands as they sang. Then Rick raised both his arms and they stopped, only to start again as he began to move. Unlike what Tanya was used to, he did not concentrate on her, but stayed in the centre of the floor, making the women slowly dance around him as he displayed his fine form and began to move ever slowly faster and the music followed him, faster and faster. Soon the girls stopped dancing and joined the crowd clapping as Rick began the deep knee bends and leg flings as the music went faster and faster. He went to his back, alternately suspending himself on one arm, leg kicking and arm raising, then jumping straight up in the air and jamming both feet rapidly down in rhythm with the music and he crashed to a stop, chest heaving with excursion. The music stopped with him.

Now he began to dance slowly, his arms out at his sides, he approached the three girls dancing around them and looking them up and down. He centred his attention on Tanya and she felt herself blush and felt her heart begin to race under her blouse and it was not an act this time when she lowered her head to avoid his glance. When he gently placed his hand around her waist she felt her legs go numb and a shiver go up her spine. She had to concentrate hard to follow his movements and at the end, when he crushed her to his chest, it was all she could do to hold herself back from grabbing his head and kissing him. It was several seconds before she realized the dance was over and she was staring up into his deep blue eyes, losing herself into their depths and that the crowd was cheering and gathering around them. Reluctantly she placed her hands on his chest and pushed herself away from him.

"Thank you for the dance Richard," she forced herself to say. "It was wonderful, but I must rejoin my comrades now."

"The pleasure was all mine Tanya and my friends call me Rick." He said.

"Thank you Rick," she said. "I hope we can meet again sometime." And she escaped before she could lose whatever control she still had.

"Ah little brother has stolen anther heart," Elizabeth said, taking his arm and placing her head on his shoulder."

"I wish," Rick said. "Not gonna happen though. She is way to up there for me. God but she is beautiful. Did you see those green eyes?"

"You must really have it bad for her brother," she said. "When all a guy notices is a girls eyes, she's got him."

"Shit all she has to do is crook her finger and I'll come running," Rick said.

Tanya felt herself tingle with a jealousy she rarely felt, as she saw the striking blond who had been dancing with them, take Ricks arm and put her head on his shoulder, then look into his eyes and speak. God I have not thought of a man like this since I was a school girl. But it can never be. He is from here and I am from there and he is obviously taken.

The next day she was on an airplane headed back home, sitting by herself in the back and thinking of what might have been.

Chapter Seven

"Alright you bone heads, quit grabbing ass and get your shit squared away, we aren't on a holiday here," Rick yelled out.

"Really," Al said, his head sticking out of his LAV. "I thought this was an all-inclusive vacation spot. You mean we have to work?"

"And I got a special hair do and everything," Julia said from the turret of Rick's LAV blowing a kiss at Al, who blushed and ducked back into his vehicle.

"Lover boy my ass," she said.

"You two an item now or what?' Rick asked.

"Oh yes," Julia said. "The dumb Jew doesn't know it yet, but he's marrying me when we get back home."

"God help us all, the two smart asses of the company getting married," Harold called up from the interior of the modified LAV.

They were back in Afghanistan, this time as part of the battalion in their normal role of reconnaissance. Canada had taken over responsibility of this part of the country and replaced the US Marines who had been here before. Already things were calmer and it was hoped that with the addition of the Regiment, that they would be more than ready for the Taliban and their summer offensives. Rick's company would be tasked with forward reconnaissance and was also tasked as the rapid response team should any of the many outposts the Canadian Army had set up, come under attack. They would not be bored, Rick thought. Harold had brought along two of the armed version of their latest toys and would be putting them through real field testing.

"Yo, Gadget," Julia called up. "Brigade wants to talk to you."

"You yahoos had better have all this shit squared away by the time I get back here or there will be no cookies and milk for you tonight," Rick yelled over his shoulder as he walked toward where the headquarters was located.

"God damn slave driver," Al yelled at his back. "Never catch a break with this guy."

"Shit if you was any slower you'd be backin' up," Bill said.

"All you Warrants is all the same," Al complained. "Almost as bad as real officers."

"I heard that," Harold said. "You might hurt my feelings if you keep talking like that."

Rick smiled to himself as he walked out of earshot. The six months of rest had done his people a world of good. He hadn't realized how tired they really were until after a few days at home. Well at least this time we get to drive around and have a lot of extra bodies with us, he thought.

"Master Warrant Bekenbaum sir," he said to the lieutenant in charge at the front desk.

"Just a moment Mr. Bekenbaum," the lieutenant said. "I will let the General and the Colonel know you are here."

The lieutenant was a member of the third battalion PPCLI, who the Regiment was nominally attached to for this deployment. They were in the middle of their rotation and the Regiment had been sent now, so that their rotation would overlap with the next battalion that came in.

A minute later and Rick was being asked to sit down. The commanding General was leaning against a window and the battalion colonel was sitting behind his desk as Rick took a spare seat.

"Master Warrant, we have a task for your people," the colonel said. "There is a friendly local warlord that we have intermittent communications failure with. We have promised them a better set up. We feel that with your electronics expertise and your multiple language skills, you are the perfect people for the job. You will be joined by a German communications team and an American communications team. Both of these teams are lightly armed and in addition to the support you will be providing them with the installation of the equipment, you will be providing security for the mission. Additionally, currently in place on the site are a small group of lightly armed Ukrainian communications people that you will provide liaison with. You will leave in three days. Questions?"

"Yes sir," Rick said. "Who is in charge and who do we report too? Also, what are the Rules of Engagement?"

"Well Major," the General said. "You are in charge and I believe your regiment's standard ROE's will be in force as usual. Coordinates for link up with the Americans, as well as your final destination, are being sent to your people as we speak and we expect the Germans to be here any time now. Oh and Major, you are out of uniform."

The general flipped a small box at Rick. "Your father sent you those, said to take care of them, they are a family heirloom. Now get out of here and get your people ready."

"Congratulations sir," the lieutenant said to a confused Rick, as he left the office and headed back to his part of the camp.

All one hundred of his troopers were lined up and at attention when a, "Officer on Deck!" was yelled out by Bill. Rick looked around for the officer then saw that the whole company was saluting him.

"If the Major would permit?" Julia said, coming up and holding her hand out for the small box in Rick's hand.

Then he saw the antique pattern Majors insignia the box held. She removed his Master Warrant insignia and placed it in the box and fastened the major's on, then took two steps backward, came to attention and saluted.

"Three cheers for Major Bekenbaum!" Bill yelled out. "Hip Hip!"

Then an embarrassed Rick was mobbed by his troopers.

"Did all you assholes know about this?" he asked.

"But of course mine commandant," Al said. "We knew about it before we left home. We were all sworn to secrecy on pain of death by General and Colonels Bekenbaum not to tell you."

"Ya and the beers on you tonight," Harold said.

"Oh shit," Rick said. "Do you guys have any idea how much Harold can drink. He's gonna make this poor farmer broke."

"Hey that's my line," Harold said.

Rick was on his third beer and starting to get a glow on, when a staff PPCLI corporal came up.

"Major, there is a German officer looking for you," the corporal said.

"Oh why not," Rick said. "Tell our good comrade and his buddies to join us. Maybe he can even buy a round."

A short time later, ten soldiers in dark green pattern camouflage entered the tent, which went quiet at their arrival. They marched up to Rick and saluted.

"Well, at least the targets will be off our backs with you guys around," Rick said, returning the salute. "By the way, we don't salute indoors. Who's the guy in charge?"

"Captain Erich von Bekenbaum with party of nine sir!" the Captain said with an Oxford accent.

"Oh my God, who let the Limey in here?" Patricia said in German.

"Did he say von?" Al said in the same language. "Hey Gadget if he's a von and he has the same last name he must be related no? Then maybe you're not payin' us enough. Bein' royalty and all."

"I'm thinking of reducing your pay you slakerd," Rick said, also in German. "My God man sit down, you are making my neck sore looking up at you. Beer or vodka? Little to early for vodka for me, but whatever. Unfortunately I'm buying, so what's another ten mouths eh?

"So Captain, you're a day early."

The captain finished his swig of beer and looked at the bottle. "This is better than the American beer," he said. "We thought we would come early so that we can better coordinate when we move out."

"Do you see you bums," Rick said. "That is what a real army does. Prepares before they move. Not like you yahoos."

"Hey I prepared all the beer," Al said. "Don't be blamin all that on me. The old Master Warrant was a little lax about things."

"Ya well I'm promoting you to Warrant Officer so you better do a good job and prove me wrong."

"Oh Christ!" Bill said. "A bloody car salesman for a Warrant."

"Almost as bad as a truck driver for a Master Warrant," Rick said. "You're promoted too."

"Aw shit, how do I transfer out of this chicken shit outfit?" Harold said.

"Hey never mind cheap skate," Al said. "Isn't it about time you bought a round?"

"No way," Harold said, sitting up straight. "Both of you just got promoted and owe us a round each. Then the new guys have to buy a round each. Why I won't have to buy until I retire at this rate."

"Until you retire?" Julia said. "When did you start working?"

"Don't mind them Captain," Rick said. "Our unit is a little different. We all grew up together."

"I myself have similar problems from time to time," the captain said. "One can never tell what the unwashed rabble will say."

"Hey speak for yourself," a large sergeant said. "I'll have you know I had a bath at Easter time."

"Ja and I had mine at Christmas," a corporal chimed in.

"Hey, how do we sign up for the Kraut Army?" Al said. "You guys get baths? I'm callin my lawyer, we're getting gyped."

"Ok that's settled then," Rick said. "You and I are both in trouble with this bunch. Can't wait to see what the Yanks throw at me. Seriously, you are not going in the field with those uniforms? I can get you some tan ones if you need them."

"No, these are our base uniforms," the Captain said. "Our vehicles are desert cammo too."

"Good that's one load off my mind," Rick said. "How much field time do you have, are you weapons qualified and what kind of vehicles do you have?"

"We have been out here for about two months now," the Captain said. "We are combat engineers and can hold our own if we have to. I have three G-Wagons, two with machine gun mounts."

"Ok," Rick said. "I'll put you in the middle of the column in between LAVs. We have a two hundred kilometre journey and with the almost non-existent roads around here, I figure two days travel to where we are going. Of course that may change depending on what the Yanks show up with. I generally send a LAV and two armed G-wagons out as scouts about half an hour before we leave. We are supposed to link up with the Yanks about noon tomorrow."

"I will have my people get your comm frequencies from you," the captain said. "Would you be related to Nicolas Bekenbaum by chance?"

"Ya he's my grandfather, why?"

"Ah well, hello then cousin," the captain said holding out his hand. "I had the pleasure of meeting General Bekenbaum, when he came to visit my father in Germany just before we left. He said to say hello if I ran into you over here."

"Is that where he ended up?' Rick said. "He took off on a long holiday after he retired and I have been pretty much deployed full time, so have been out of touch. So we are related then?"

"Oh yes, in fact you could have the von as well," Erich said.

"Ah, all that crap is no big deal where we come from," Rick said. "Maybe you could come and visit someday. My folks and sister would like to meet some of the old country relatives we have been hearing about."

"My troop and I are scheduled for training next September with you people," Erich said. "It was a very tough competition to qualify for."

"Oh, you ain't seen nothing yet Erich." Rick said. "Ok you reprobates, enough party, back to work. I wanna be out of here by daybreak."

"Bloody slave driver," Al said. "Are your officers just as bad?"

"Oh sometimes the Captain is much worse," a sergeant said. "Why one time he even made me work on a Sunday."

"That would be grounds for a mutiny in our Army," Patricia said. "You have more restraint than we do."

"I have a feeling you guys will fit right in." Rick said to Erich, as the troopers filled out to finish their preparations for the next day.

The sun was barely over the horizon, when Rick signalled the lead vehicle to proceed. The scouts had left an hour earlier. Four of the LAVs had in addition to their regular equipment, a ten foot section of antenna mast strapped on it and the convoy made its way out of the gate and accelerated up the road, the Germans tucked in between LAVs. Their G-wagons loaded down with cable and wire on the roofs. It was just before noon when they reached the rendezvous point, formed a laager with the G-wagons in the centre and stopped for lunch.

It was two o'clock, when Julia came up to Rick who was laying on the top of the LAV, his shirt off, boonie hat down over his eyes, head leaned against the turret having a snooze.

"Yanks aren't showing up until tomorrow noon now Gadget," she said.

"Fucking knew it," he said. "Ok, deploy the remotes and have Bill come and see me. Harold, get one of the birds up and take a look around. Oh ya, let the Krauts know too."

"Yanks are a no show eh?" Bill said. "What?" Rick had raised his eyebrows. "Just cause I was born there don't make me one."

"If you say so," Rick said. "Ok, I want the remote sensors, all of them, deployed. Harold is going to take a look around with a drone. Quarter watch starting now. We are out here exposed and I don't need any surprises. Captain, if I can have your people man one of our out posts with one of your guns? Have your Sergeant coordinate with the Master Warrant here. Hopefully our Allies will be here tomorrow. Otherwise I am leaving without them."

"You would do that?" Erich said.

"It's my mission, they snooze they lose," Rick said. "Break out the cammo, no sense in making it easy for them."

A high pitched engine noise started at the rear of the LAV rising in tempo and the drone rattled away until it became airborne and started to climb away.

"That is a different design," Erich said.

"Ya, it's one of our proto types," Rick said. "It's only got a 5.62 mini gun mounted right now."

"Only!" Erich said.

"Ya we can also mount six rockets on it," Rick said. "Worked ok back home."

"I'll bet," Erich said.

Harold was manipulating the controls while watching a colour monitor fed from the front camera on the drone. Four other monitors were showing the right, left and rear down looking views and the fourth was pointing straight down.

"Those monitors are being monitored by the command LAVs," Rick said. "We have two drones with us. Sandy will operate the second one from her command LAV and another will take over this ones monitors. We have run under battle training conditions. Even while moving we were able to utilize the units to full capacity. The pilot will also target and destroy targets when required."

"You say this is a proto type?"

"Yes, if it works ok, we will produce about a hundred to deploy and sell ourselves and then licence it out," Rick said.

"I think our company may be interested if it works," Erich said.

"Oh I think grandpa is way ahead of you there Erich," Rick said. "We are big shareholders of your company already if it's the company I am thinking of."

They passed an uneventful night and at 13:00 Rick sent his scouts out and had the others prepare to move. Just before he gave the order to move, Harold spotted the American column in the distance with the drone. It was a column of six HUMVs, one of which was a supply vehicle. Rick gave the order to move out at 14:00.

"Julia, contact that American commander and have him catch us up," Rick ordered as Patricia put the LAV in gear and moved out.

"He wants to talk to you sir," she said.

"Unit calling Bravo One, go ahead," Rick said after Julia patched him in.

"Bravo One this is Godfather Six Actual, how read over?"

"Godfather Six, cut the crap, what do you need?"

"Bravo One, Godfather Six Actual, can I speak with your commander?"

"Godfather six, you must have been asleep during your briefing. This is Bravo One. I repeat what do you need?"

"Uh roger Bravo One. My people have been on the road for three hours and could use a break. It is our SOP, over."

"Well Godfather Six, it is my SOP to leave on time and I have. My people have been waiting for you since noon yesterday. You have put my schedule behind by twenty four hours already. I plan on moving a hundred K by the end of the day and my scouts are an hour ahead of me as we speak. Take as many breaks as you want. You are on your own until you link up with me over."

"Ah, Bravo One this is Godfather Six, I am a column of six HUMVs and need support sir."

"Well, the sooner you catch us up, the sooner you have support Godfather Six. If there is nothing else of importance, Bravo One out."

"I don't want to talk to that yahoo again unless it's an emergency Julia."

"Idiot thinks he's still on maneuvers State side," Harold said. "Oh, looks like he got the picture, they're booting it."

"Tell them to slot in behind the G-wagons when they catch us up Julia and I want to see that Godfather Six and his officers and senior NCO's ASAP after we laager for the night."

Rick was just climbing down from his LAV when the American Captain came rushing forward. Hastily waved a hand at his helmeted head and stuck out his hand.

"Captain Whitaker, Force Recon US Marines Major, I can't tell you how pleased....."

"Godfather Six," Rick said, not returning the salute or taking the preferred hand. "In my army, when a commanding officer gives an order to report to him, it is expected to be followed only after making sure his people are properly deployed and looked after and has actually got something to report. Do you see any of my people here? Now get back to your troops and report back to me in the proper manner."

"Julia, Pat, see if we know any of these people later on and get a feel for this Godfather Six and the rest of the officers."

One by one, the Canadian vehicle commanders gathered by the command LAV, most of them with coffee cups in hand. The four Germans were next. Last came the seven Americans. Bill called them to attention and without preliminaries Rick started.

"We are a day behind schedule and still have a hundred and fifty k to go. We are at the beginning of bad guy country and most of the travel will be off road, so we will make a hundred K tomorrow, if we leave at dawn. Bill?"

"Perimeter is set. Remotes are being deployed and tested. I have the HUMVs on an inside perimeter, plugging the gaps and the G- wagons inside that. I think cammo netting will be a waste of time and recommend a twenty five percent watch at this time."

"Ya, the bad guys already know we are here and how we are deployed, netting is a waste of time," Rick said. "Harold, how much time do you have left?"

"About an hour," Harold said. "So far so good. Sandy will take over tonight and tomorrow with hers as soon as we are done here."

"Erich?"

"Nothing to report Major. Machines and men in good order. We have the third foot watch."

"Godfather Six?"

"My men and machines are tired sir. We will need until at least until ten hundred before we will be able to move and I request we be relieved of the twenty five percent watch requirement."

"And I requested not to have you people involved in this mission, but was over ridden Godfather Six. You will leave when we do tomorrow or be left behind. You will maintain twenty five percent watch or we will not protect you in the future. This is the real war Godfather Six, not some pretend exercise State side. People die out here if they don't stay alert."

"Lieutenant are your people or machines unfit for duty?" Rick singled out a young first lieutenant from the Marines.

"No sir, my people and equipment are up to standard and ready for anything sir!"

"You will be able to maintain a twenty five percent watch and your share of foot patrol and still be ready and alert tomorrow?"

"Yes sir! Recon sir!"

"Semper Phi lieutenant, outstanding. Ok people, get some grub and some sleep. Early day tomorrow. Godfather Six, a moment."

"You are an Annapolis grad Captain?"

"Yes sir," he said.

"And I suppose a posting to Force Recon will enhance your career?"

"Yes sir."

"I apologize for singling you out in front of the others just now. I am newly promoted from the ranks and forget myself, it will not happen again. Now as things stand, I choose not to know your name. The reason why, is that until I am proved otherwise, I do not think you will survive this mission. Either the enemy will kill you, or I or one of my men will. You should not be here Godfather Six. You do not have the skills for it and are going to get my people killed. If you were smart, you would rely on your NCO's and that young lieutenant and you might, just might come out of this alive. Dismissed Godfather Six Actual."

"Hey Bill what's up, you got me some decent coffee there?" Rick said watching the Marine Captain walk away.

"I see you had a little chat with Mr. Wonderful eh?" Bill said, handing Rick a cup of rum laced coffee.

"Ah just what the doctor ordered," Rick said taking a tentative sip of the coffee. "Well Gunny good to see you again. What can you tell me about your gang?"

"It's been a long time sir," the Gunnery Sergeant said. "You was just a dumb recruit the last time we met."

"Ya, me and that dumb recruit had you by the balls that night and you know it John," Bill said.

"You got that right, kicked our asses good. Was that really you guys here last fall?"

"Far as I know it was some guys by the name of Smith and Wesson." Rick said, taking a deeper pull of his coffee.

"Ya sure, a big black buck named Wesson and a way to cute black honey named Smith. A smart ass called Al, a way too cute blond named Julia and a smart ass Master Warrant named Rick Smith. I was born at night, but not last night. They had us out all the month of December looking for you guys."

"I really don't know what you are talking about John," Rick said. "But I hear you got within five hundred meters of them at one point.

The SEALS were right beside them talking to them, dumb asses that they are."

"Shit, I told the lieutenant I could smell horses. But oh no, he knew better. God damn it, we almost had you."

"Almost don't cut it John. Now what's with this Godfather Six guy?" Rick said.

"Ticket Puncher," John said. "His pop is some big shot. Runs some big company that makes drones for us. I'd be careful, he's got a lot of pull. He's pretty harmless, we mostly ignore him."

"I don't have time for that crap," Rick said. "Teach him his job, because if he gets in my way he is going to get killed and I told him that. What about the rest of them?"

"Half of them have completed your program including the kid. They'll do."

"Ok, if you say so John. Do you know you snore at night? And I can't believe you still undo your boot laces even after what I did to you in training."

"Goddamn it, I knew it was you assholes! I suppose it was this big black asshole who stole the lieutenants GPS too?"

"GPS? What's a GPS," Bill said, passing the bottle.

The next morning, the Marines were ready to go with the rest of the group and John was speaking with the Captain, pointing things out to him and the Captain was actually listening.

Having nothing to do but listen to the droning of the engine, or watch Harold's monitors, Rick soon dropped off to sleep. He had spent half the night patrolling the lines, talking with troopers and getting a feel for the German and American troops. They would do he thought.

"Gadget, hey Gadget," Julia was tugging on his foot. "I'm picking up a real faint broad cast in Russian on our old frequency."

"Patch me in," Rick said. "Hey Bill, do me a favour and let the antennae loose will you?"

They usually traveled with the antennae tied down to the hull of the LAV to lessen the chance of them being seen. But it also limited radio reception at times.

"Any station, any station, Uniform Four declaring an emergency. Any station, any station, Uniform Four declaring an emergency," Rick heard faintly on his head set. The voice was female and talking in Ukrainian.

"Uniform Four, this is Bravo One, read you two by three. State your emergency, over."

"Bravo One, Uniform Four. We have you eight by eight. Our position is under attack by superior force, with mortars, RPG and heavy machine guns. We have casualties and running low on ammunition over."

"What's your location Uniform Four?"

"Shit that's where we are supposed to install this radio equipment," Rick said after he had the coordinates. "Can you raise home base?"

"No we are to far away and to low," Julia said. "I can get sat comms tonight, but otherwise we are SOL."

"Uniform Four, we are a light armoured column about twelve hours from your location. We have no comms to HQ until tonight. Is it possible for you to use your high power set?"

"Negative Bravo One. The comms were taken out the first day and radio personnel killed."

"Harold get the other bird ready, have Sandy send hers to that local and set up surveillance until you get there, then have her come back and refuel."

"We are on our way Uniform Four hang in there. Conserve your batteries as much as possible."

"Roger Bravo One. Attackers usually take the night off. We should be ok for another couple of days."

"Roger Uniform Four. Bravo will monitor this frequency."

"Bravo One, Uniform Four out."

"Shit it never rains but it pours." Rick said. "Patch me into command net and keep monitoring this one."

"Bravo One to task force," Rick said. *"Our destination is under heavy attack, has taken casualties and is running low on ammunition. We are the closest units for relief. Comms are down until tonight and by then we will definitely be closer than even any chopper relief. We will relieve our allies people. Task force is to increase speed to best possible speed. Bravo screen, increase speed and keep vigilant. Little bird will be overhead shortly to assist you. Stand five klicks short of target. It going to get rough people and it's going to be a long day. Bravo one out."*

"Crank it up Pat."

It was almost midnight when they finally stopped, five kilometres short of their final destination. There had been no sight of enemy along the way, nor was there any until the target itself.

"Uniform Four, Bravo One over."

"Bravo One, Alpha One. Uniform Four is passed out. She has been up for thirty six hours."

"Alpha One, Bravo One, how you holding up?"

"We have enough ammunition to repel one more attack Bravo One, barely."

"We are not far away Alpha One. We have surveillance set up and are making an attack plan as we speak. When does Taliban start operations?"

"After morning prayers. So far they are just hitting us from the front Bravo One. Very unimaginative."

"Ok Alpha One, expect us shortly after dawn with massive shock and awe. You won't miss us."

"I knew my friend Master Warrant Rick would not let me down."

"That you Bashir, you old scoundrel?"

"Yes my friend Rick, it is I Bashir. I told my people you would come, now I will tell them you have and God is truly with us now."

"Well don't count your chickens before they hatch Bashir. I only have a hundred and fifty people and we are looking at over a thousand bad guys with heavy weapons. But we will do our best."

"I will pray for the Taliban dead to be, friend Rick"

"Ok Bashir. Now I want you to change to this frequency," Rick gave him a new set of numbers. *"The rest of my people cannot monitor the one we are on now. You have your people ready at dawn. We are coming. Bravo One out."*

"Well Julia baby can we get any help?"

"Not a chance Gadget, we are on our own. All air assets are committed."

"Ok meeting in five."

"Hey boss," Harold said. "The Yanks have a couple of Mark fours about fifty kliks from here."

"Got a back door?" Rick asked.

"Oh ya. They've got two missiles each."

"Do it."

"Say good night US Air Force. Got em Boss."

"Ok task them to somebody else Harold, I need you and Sandy on ours."

Rick and his four LAVs were just below a hill five hundred yards from the enemy flank. All of the infantry had been dismounted and were lining the crest of the hill. Another four LAVs were on the other side with their infantry, with the last two backing up the HUMVs and G-Wagons to the rear. Everyone was waiting for Ricks signal.

"Break out the colours Julia," Rick ordered.

"They're gonna see them," Julia said.

"That's the point," Rick said. "I want them to know who's killing them this time."

Julia clambered to the top of the LAV and attached half sized versions of the national and regimental flags to the tops of the two antennae's at the rear of the vehicle. The Maple Leaf on the right and the blue, yellow and red with the Eagle and Bear flanking the maple leaf in the middle on the left.

One by one, the other three LAVs followed suit and Rick nodded. For the first time for a long time, the Regiment would go to war under their own colours.

Rick could hear the prayers finishing on the other side of the hill and looked down at Harold's monitors and saw the enemy deploying to their attack positions.

"You ready Harold?"

"Anytime Boss."

"Bravo One to Bravo task force. All units to place comms on intercom, volume set on high."

"When somebody fucks with a friend of the Eagle and the Bear, they Fuck with the Eagle and the Bear," Ricks voice in English came blaring across the landscape.

"I am Richard, Son of Paul, son of Nicolas, son of John, son of Andreas, clan of Bekenbaum, fourth Earl of Didsbury. What is done to General Bashir Khan and his people is done to me and mine. So say I before God and Man!"

"So say we all!" came the massed voices of the Regiment. Rick waved his arm into the LAV and the Regimental song began to blare across the country side. The voices joined it, singing in Russian. Faster and faster the song came and taking a quick glance at the monitors, Rick saw Taliban fighters standing and turning in circles, trying to locate the source of the noise.

"Now!" Rick yelled at Harold and the sky came alive as the drones let go with their rockets at the heavy machine gun and mortar crews in time to the songs climax. An eerie silence fell over the landscape as the explosions and the song stopped. Then Rick grabbed the handles of his fifty calibre machine gun and yelled, "Ok Julia let 'er rip!"

The country side erupted to the Immigrant Song by Led Zeppelin and Pat gunned the engine and dropped in gear, the LAV cresting the hill every gun blazing just as the words, we come from the land of Ice and Snow, were blaring out. Julia had the twenty millimetre canon blasting at targets and the turret constantly in motion, while Rick was raking his fifty cal across lines of shocked enemy who did not know which way to turn. The infantry was standing, every gun blazing. LAVs on both sides spitting death at anything that moved and the HUMVs and G=Wagons firing as they ran in from the rear. Harold and Sandy made runs with the drones spitting death from the skies with their mini guns. There was nowhere for the enemy to hide and they died in their hundreds. Soon there were no more targets and the firing stopped and once again silence ruled the landscape.

Then the cheering started. It started first on the battlements of the walled town and soon spread to the field, as troopers let their emotions run loose. Rick looked to the battlements and saw a large blue, yellow and red flag flying high and straight out on a high flag pole. It had a Bear on the right and an Eagle on the left, but no maple leaf in the centre and suddenly Rick knew. As all the members of the regiment who began to look knew and they stopped their cheering and only looked. They looked at their original colour. The rest of the task force slowly stopped cheering as they saw the Canadians come together and off of their LAVs to stare at the flag.

Then came an explosion and a drone spun out of control. Rick spun his fifty cal around and saw the man toss his RPG launcher away and stitched him with the fifty, blowing him in half.

"Shit, Sandy!" Rick yelled, as he dove off the turret and sprinted to the burning vehicle. Troopers were already hauling out the occupants when Rick got there and other troopers were now shooting at anything that still moved in the kill zone. She was still alive when he slid to a stop beside her and cradled her head on his lap.

"Sorry Gadget. I let you down," she said.

"No, you did good Twinky, you did good." Rick said, tears running down his cheeks.

"We had fun eh Gadget? We showed those assholes not to fuck with us eh?"

Rick ripped out his syringe of morphine from his belly pack and jabbed it into her arm, giving her the full dose.

She shut her eyes for a few seconds, then opened them back up again as Rick was stroking her hair.

"You know, our folks really wanted us to hook up Rick," she said.

"Ya I know Sandy, I know." Rick said.

"You were the best friend I ever had and I love you like a brother Rick."

"I know Sandy and I love you as I love my own sister."

"You tell that lunk of a husband of mine, I miss him and love him like crazy. And you tell my kids I love them and that mommy will be with them always."

Rick held his hand out as another spasm of pain gripped her and Harold gave him anther syringe of Morphine.

"If you can, bury me beside my great, great grandmother Rick, please? It can't be far from here."

She looked above Ricks head and said. "And you, you broke his heart when you left him the last time. He loves you and I know you love him. If you don't marry him, I promise to make your life a living hell." And Sandy smiled. "Men know nothing of these things, you have to push them along, especially the Bekenbaum men."

"Now, Rick, give me the last one, it is time and I don't want to die screaming in pain." She dug out her own Morphine syringe and gave it to Rick. "You know it has to be. Here I will help you."

She took his hand and placed it on her arm and helped him push the needle in. She died with a smile on her face. As Rick smoothed her hair into place he felt a gentle hand on his shoulder. He looked around and straight into Tanya's deep green eyes.

"Uniform Four?" Rick asked and she nodded. "Thank God we got here in time!" he stood, nodded his head and moved away, yelling orders as he did..

Chapter Eight

"*Eagle, Eagle, this is Charley One.*"

"*Charley One, Eagle Six, secure line.*"

"*At 06:00 local, Charley engaged Taliban force threatening to overwhelm our missions position. Estimated Taliban dead one thousand five hundred. Charley casualties as follows. One Command LAV destroyed. Five KIA, no WIA. Captain Sandra von Hoaedle has requested to be interned locally beside her ancestor, that request has been granted by the local authorities. The other KIA will be repatriated home. Local force suffered one hundred WIA and ten KIA. Forces of the Ukraine, five KIA, no WIA. Names to follow. List of expended and destroyed ammunition and arms to follow. Copy?*"

"*Major, hold off on the captain's funeral. The Regiment will be present. Are you ok?*"

"*Yes general, I am fine.*"

"*Do the troops need relief?*"

"*No sir. And the troops and I mean all of the troops, will refuse relief if it comes.*"

"*Are you sure?*"

"*All of the troops have informed their commands that they will stay by us until we leave general.*"

"*Ok, son. We will be airborne in four hours and local transport is being arranged. You will be relieved after the funeral, is that clear?*"

"*Yes sir.*"

"*Ok, I will have Sandy's family with us when we arrive. Give my best to General Khan and if he needs anything you be sure to let me know.*"

"Thanks pop, I will."

"Company meeting in an hour Bill," Rick said as he hung up the sat phone. "I think the locals can handle security for a while. Ask the Gunny and Captain Whitmore to join me at their convenience."

"Sit down Gentlemen," Rick said to the two Marines as they entered his tent.

"Your Colonel was very upset with me when I told him of your involvement in this engagement." Rick said. "I reminded him of my ROE's and that you were following my orders and that no blame, if there is any, will laid at your door step. Your people did extremely well and the gunny tells me you did well yourself captain Whitmore. Was this your first look at the elephant?"

"Yes sir. I was scared out of my mind sir and I think I might have pissed myself."

"So did I Cap," the Gunny said. "But oh what a sight you guys made coming over that hill. Flags flying and guns blazing. Just like a cavalry charge in the old days."

"Ya it was fun, wasn't it?" Rick said. "Much better than surviving on half rations for three months behind enemy lines."

"I'm sorry about your losses Major," the captain said. "I wish we could have stopped it, but we didn't see it until it was to late."

"Take it as a lesson Whitmore," Rick said. "I lost control of the situation and five of my people died because of it. In the grand scheme, I suffered under five percent losses, but I grew up with those five percent and it hurts. I have to go home and see their parents and their siblings. This I have to live with."

"My father is calling yours Whitmore and he is telling him I am pleased with your performance. The Gunny tells me you are progressing well. I hope you continue. Please tell your people well done."

"Major, the regiment is waiting." Bill said.

"I will be with you shortly," Rick said. "Gentlemen please join your troops."

Rick walked out of the tent and surveyed the troopers. His were in the middle, flanked on the right by the Germans and the left by the Americans. They were all at attention and saluted at the command of the Master Warrant. Rick returned the salute and stood, still struggling with something to say.

He went to one knee and made the sign of the cross and the assembled troops followed suit, the Catholics making the sign of the cross as well.

"Father, thank you for our victory and our health today. Thank you for giving us the wisdom to defeat our enemy and for the wisdom of our trainers and our weapons makers for providing us with the tools to do our jobs well. We ask you to look out for the families of our and our enemies dead and to help them with their sorrow. We ask your forgiveness for the deaths of your children. I ask you to hold my troopers blameless as it was my decisions they acted on. Any fault is mine and mine alone. Finally, I ask you to take my fallen comrades into your bosom as they did what they thought best to save the innocent from harm."

He made the sign of the cross again and stood.

"In a few hours, we are going to be swamped with brass, government officials and world press," Rick said. "We have only these few hours to savour what we have accomplished here. We have only these few hours to come to terms with the grief of losing comrades and lifelong friends. It is especially hard in a regiment like ours where we have lived together for generations and in many cases are related to each other. The five that died I went to school with. I went to basic with, I served with, not only here, but in other areas of operation. Sandy and I had a special relationship. Her family and mine have been close, right from the beginning. One of her ancestors was the sister of one of mine. Another was the mother of another famous ancestor and the wife of another and buried not far from here. Her husband is a cousin to my sister's husband, who was himself killed, a hero in Iraq. Sandy was the head cheerleader of our class in high school. She was my business partner and it was she who developed some of the most sophisticated software the world has ever seen to operate our drone aircraft. She was a devoted mother of two, a loving wife, a dear friend and a deadly and dedicated warrior. One of her last words were, 'We showed those assholes not to fuck with us eh?'"

Rick pointed to the battlefield, with the still smouldering LAV and the enemy lying where they fell.

"Those idiots felt they could kill our friends. They felt they could rule the world and impose their draconian principles on us all! If they were allowed to be in control, Sandy would never have been allowed to function at her best potential. Your mothers and sisters and wives, would have no rights as human beings. They call us infidels. Mongrels. Well we are. And us Mongrels kicked their fucking asses!

"Our Regimental moto is Determination Against All Odds. Once again we were outnumbered ten to one. Once again with superior weaponry, superior training and most of all superior will, we destroyed those who dare stand against us.

"The last time we stood on this field of battle, we had the help of German and English Allies. Today, we had the help of German and American Allies. That help was crucial. Captain von Bekenbaum and Captain Whitmore and their troops were pivotal in closing the last escape route for those turkeys. In their unarmored vehicles, they showed as much courage as we in the main assault. As Gunny Alfardson said, 'Christ, banners flying, guns blazing, it was like a cavalry charge of old.'

"And it was people. It was just like a cavalry charge of old, because at root, at our heart, that's what we are. We are cavalry, we are recon. We are the fucking Bears and Eagles! And we kicked some serious fucking ass!"

Rick stood with his fists rammed into his hips looking over his troops who stood in silence, then raised his right fist in the air above his head and yelled at the top of his lungs and it was the signal they were waiting for. The whole group yelled and punched their fists in the air and grabbed one another in hugs and handshakes. This went on for several minutes and was interrupted by a single loud gunshot.

Rick looked behind him. Approaching from behind the walls, was a solid wall of people. Young and old. Male and female. Most had rifles on their shoulders, from AKs to Lee Enfields to antique bolt action single shot carbines and even Winchester rifles. They were led by Bashir and as they came, they fanned out in lines behind and to each side of him. As he walked toward them he shook out the flag he was carrying so that it caught the breeze and the faded cloth revealed the light blue, yellow, red with the Bear on the right and the Eagle on the left. The group marched to within ten yards of the assembled company and stopped. Bashir planting the flag staff firmly in the ground so that the flag stood by itself, proud and flying free.

"Once before, your people came to us," Bashir said. "Once before a great leader came among us and delivered us from Tyranny. Once before, a mighty Bekenbaum came. He said then, ask and we shall return. We asked, you returned. Whatever we are, what we have become is because of that great man. We heeded his words and became powerful, rich and fruitful.

"Richard, when we worked together so many months ago, you did not know who we were and at first we did not know who you were. But we soon learned and we did not tell you. When we were calling for help, we did not know it was you who were coming to our aide. My friends, God has had His hand in this. Andreas Bekenbaum, gave us this flag. We moved our settlement to this place. This place, a sacred place, where three thousand of you killed ten thousand of them, to give us our freedom and a new way of life."

Bashir pointed at the battlefield.

"One hundred and thirty years ago, your people, on this very field, gave us our freedom and today on this same field you have given it to us again. This morning, Earl Bekenbaum, you gave us your oath. Now I, give you ours."

Bashir walked up to Rick, knelt and placed his rifle at Ricks feet. He took Ricks hands and placed his own inside them and bowed his head.

"I Bashir Khan, leader of my people and with the support of my people say. I am Bashir, what is done to Earl Bekenbaum or his, is done to me and mine. So say I in front of God and man."

"So say we all!" his massed people said.

Bashir stood and Rick extended his hand. "You didn't have to do that," he said.

"Yes Earl Bekenbaum, I did." Bashir said. "It is a point of honour and I have bound my clan to yours. We did it freely and without coercion."

"Well, Bashir, my name is Rick, not Earl Bekenbaum, not to my friends. Oh and let's keep this Earl stuff among us eh?"

"I might have a problem with that Major," Captain Whitmore said. "I have a member of the press embedded with me."

"Ah shit!" Rick said. "Where is he?" Whitmore pointed to a man whose uniform was slightly different than the other Marine uniforms. "Bashir, how 'bout we let our people celebrate for bit without us? Whitmore, bring that press yahoo to my tent."

"Coffee?" Rick asked Bashir.

"Only if this is in it," Bashir dug out a mickey bottle of rum from his pocket and pored a generous amount in each coffee cup. They toasted each other and took a sip.

"You have made everyone in my clan rich Rick," Bashir said. "That last bunch, you gave us ten million US dollars."

"Holy shit," Rick said. "I had no idea. They'll be no living with Al now."

"There may be some value among those down there as well. My people will be going through the bodies any time now. We need to have that done before CIA gets here. How long do you think?"

"Another hour, two at the most."

Bashir whistled and Akmed poked his head in the tent.

"We have an hour. Get everyone involved. Every tick of paper we can find before CIA takes it all."

As Akmed left, Whitmore and the press man entered.

"Captain you stay," Rick said. "You neglected to report you had a member of the press with you. And you sir, did not report yourself to me. I could have you banned for life for this."

"I am sorry Major, the opportunity never presented itself," the reporter said.

"Papers," Rick said, holding out his hand.

He glanced over the documents quickly and handed them back.

"Unlike in America, military operations are covered under the Official Secrets Act in Canada and this is a Canadian led operation, thus you are covered under this act. You are subject to fines and imprisonment should you publish anything that we feel will jeopardize this or future operations. Is that understood?"

"But I can publish anything to do with an American unit," the man protested.

"That American unit was under my control and as such is part of the Canadian Army at that point, sorry.

"You are a freelance journalist with AP credentials Mr. Adaman. You have heard of Emily Hershmire I assume?"

"Hell yes, who hasn't? She was one, if not the best, war correspondent of her time. We are taught about her in school. Her father was a powerful industrialist and member of congress. She married a Canadian I believe. Oh don't tell me."

"Yes Mr. Adaman, she is my mother," Rick said. "It may not be in your professional best interest to piss me off. I also believe Captain Whitmore's father may take an interest in what is happening here. It may be wise to tread carefully.

"So to remove any confusion from your mind. I would appreciate it if no mention of my title or the oaths that were exchanged between my people and Bashir's were made. No mention of any previous clandestine operations were made. Those may be covered under your Home Land Security laws, in fact I am sure they are. Any mention of my regiment should be limited to 'The Canadians'. We like to keep a low profile. I would appreciate mention of Sandy, but her contributions to the drone project is Top Secret in both our countries. The contribution of our Ukrainian and German allies should also be mentioned. And it goes without saying the heroic defence of Bashir's people against overwhelming odds. Surrounded by hostile Taliban with no hope of escape and dwindling ammunition should be mentioned. These people should be admired for their tenacity and embracing social change."

"Sir the exclusion of what you want will in no way affect what I report," the reporter said. "It might add a little colour, but my God, what a display! Hell I ran out of battery and I myself took up a rifle and fired some rounds. Jesus! I think it important to mention the past history here as well. How a people returned to help their former friends is important."

"Yes Rick, I think this is wise as well," Bashir said. "My people need to know we have friends, long term friends, in the West."

"My mother will be here in two days'" Rick said. "It may be wise to collaborate that part of the story with her. I will give you exclusive access to the funeral as well."

"Hell Major, you have just made me a rich man," the reporter said and stuck out his hand.

Rick shook it as did Bashir. "As you know it is customary to seal a deal such as this with a toast. Unfortunately, Bashir's religion prohibits some things, but we can seal the deal with coffee no?"

"Ah Captain von Bekenbaum, just in time," Rick said as the rum laced coffee was being poured. "We have just concluded negotiations with Mr. Adaman here regarding what he will report in his press release. The Captain and his troops were pivotal in this operation. Well you were with them, so you saw them in action. It's time the German people had some good press you think?"

"I forgot about that!" Adaman said. "Holy shit, I'm going to be a house hold name worldwide."

Rick smiled and raised his cup. "Gentlemen, to our agreement and a successful operation."

He and Bashir laughed long and hard as the other three took a deep draught of the coffee and choked on the stiff rum.

"I forgot to warn you that Afghan coffee is strong," Rick said. "Refills?"

It was three hours before a fleet of Chinooks descended on them.

"Jesus Christ, what a show Major!" the American commanding General said, pounding Rick on the back. "Right out of Hollywood. Your birds gave a full panorama colour picture in real time of what was going on and the Goddamn audio was a stroke of genius. CNN has been broadcasting the scene of your LAVs cresting that hill continuously."

The first group of helicopters took off to be replaced with another. This time when the ramps dropped, garishly armoured members of the press sprinted off the helicopters and towards where Ricks LAVs were parked.

"Master Warrant!" Rick yelled at the top of his lungs. "You keep those God damn people out of my perimeter! Shoot 'em if you have to!"

Bill responded by jumping up to the turret of the nearest LAV, cocking the handle of its turret mounted fifty calibre and letting loose with a half dozen rounds in the direction of the battle field.

"Stop right there!" he said over the LAVs loudspeaker system. "This is still a war zone and there may be snipers around."

"Mr. Adaman," Rick said. "Please inform your brethren that you are our official press spokesman and that we will have a press conference shortly. Ask them to stay out of our way until then would you?"

"Look General, thanks for the accolades, but we still have a lot of work to do. We have to police up the battlefield. General Bashir's people have a large number of wounded and their buildings need refurbishing. My people all have remedial medical training, but his people need more than that. Can we get some of them out on these choppers and to some help?"

"I'm doing better than that Major," the general pointed at the other group coming out of the latest helicopters. These had large medical kits with them. "I'm bringing the hospital to them. Within an hour the MASH unit will be fully operational. They are your folks by the way. If you don't mind, I want to meet your fine troops. Mine will take over security from here Major."

It was a long day as Rick conveyed the general and his command staff around the battle ground, giving descriptions of the enemy positions and his staging area. How he had developed his plan. The positions of his dismounted troops was self-evident from the amount of expended brass casings lying about.

"We don't have a lot of ammo left general," Rick said. "We weren't expecting a major assault and only had minimum combat loads aboard."

"You kidding me?" the general said. "You did all this with minimal loads?"

"We are taught from a young age about fire discipline general," Rick said. "So are the Marines."

Their every move was shadowed by the press, who Ricks troopers kept at bay with menacing looks and ever present C7's at the ready.

The last stop was a tour of Bashir's defences and the general once again was impressed.

"Alright, I think we have kept the press waiting long enough," the general said. "General is there a place where we can have a dog and pony show?"

"Yes," Bashir said. "We have it set up already."

"Well let's get this circus over with then."

As they entered the room prepared for the press conference, Rick saw Tanya, still dressed like the rest of them, in the messed and wrinkled uniform she had worn for the battle.

"General," Bashir said. "I would like to introduce Major Helenchuk of the Ukraine defence force. She and her people were a very big part of our defence and especially with establishing communications with Bravo Task Force. Without her and her people's expertise, I am afraid Bravo would have arrived here much to late."

Tanya shook hands with the general and his staff, but after that kept her eyes on Rick.

The general sat down and motioned Bashir to sit on his right and Rick on his left. Tanya sat next to Bashir and Whitmore next to her, while von Bekenbaum sat next to Rick. They sat patiently while the press people filed in and sat down. Sound technicians and camera men set up their equipment and finally they were ready to begin and the cameras began to roll.

"At approximately 07:00," the General said. "Task Force Bravo began an assault that overwhelmingly defeated a vastly superior enemy, coming to the relief of our Afghan allies. Let there be no doubt ladies and gentlemen of what would have happened should they have failed. The people of this community would have been murdered to the last man, woman and child. The Taliban had stated as much in their press release yesterday. Major Bekenbaum deployed his troops with cunning and executed his plan with the audacity and bravery that we have come to expect from our Canadian friends. Ladies and gentlemen I give you Major Richard Bekenbaum."

"First let me introduce our team," Rick began. "To my left is Captain Erich von Bekenbaum of the Bundeswier, Republic of Germany. On my far right is Captain Whitmore, Force Recon United Sates Marine Corp. to his right is Major Tanya Halenchuck, Republic of Ukraine Defence Force. To her right is General Bashir Kahn, Republic of Afghanistan Defence Force. Let there be no doubt ladies and gentlemen, this was a United Nations effort.

"At 19:00 local yesterday, we received a very faint distress call from Major Helenchuck asking for assistance. Even with our sophisticated communications systems we had a hard time receiving it. Luckily, one of my team members could understand Ukrainian and we were able to establish what was going on. I had my drone commander, Captain Sandra von Hoadle, send her drone to set up surveillance of the site and we drove all night to our staging position and with consultation with Captains Whitmore and Von Bekenbaum, I was able to plan our next moves and we were in our jump off positions by 04:00 this morning. Captain von Hoadle had landed her drone by then and armed it as did Captain Harold Hassman his and they took up a holding pattern above the battlefield. During that time, Captain von Hoadle was able to establish a very tenuous communication with the United States Air force and they contributed the two armed drones they had in the area to our attack.

"At 07:00, the enemy had finished their morning prayers and were about to commence offensive operations when we launched our assault. In a short period of time, we were able to be in control of the field of battle and had inflicted heavy casualties on the enemy suffering minimal casualties of our own. One of whom was Captain Sandra von Hoadle, wife and mother of two.

"The first casualties of the action were suffered by Major Helenchuk's people. Four of her people were killed in the opening of the enemies attack, when then enemy took out the communications centre they were working in with mortars and RPGs, killing all four instantly. General Bashir's people and the remaining Ukrainians, kept the enemy at bay for two days before establishing contact with us. They had run out of heavy and light machine gun rounds, mortar and RPG rounds, had minimal AK ammunition left and in many cases were left to fight with whatever weapons were to hand. Antique bolt action black powder rifles, Winchester repeating rifles, Lee Enfield rifles from the first and second wars. They were prepared to defend themselves to the last person with bayonet, lance, sword and knife. This is the reason we are here. These people want our way of life, have embraced our way of life and were willing to die for it. Could we do any less?"

The room was silent after Rick stopped speaking. A female member of the press, at the back and with a Canadian television networks logo on her jacket stood and began to clap. It was not very long before the rest of the media joined her, giving them a standing ovation. The General stood himself, followed by Bashir and Tanya and finally Whitmore and Erich all facing Rick who stayed seated. After a time the general raised his hands and motioned everyone to sit.

"General, when did HQ become aware of what was going on?" a CNN reporter blurted out.

"We began receiving telemetry and video from the Canadian drones, just before the attack. This was followed by real time audio. Basically about the same time you did at CNN. This is a remote area and Bravos initial task was to install long range communications equipment here. Thank God they were on route or the result would have been much different."

That allowed the flood gates to open and the room was filled with reporters yelling questions.

Rick stood and put his hands on his hips which quieted the room down. He pointed at the Canadian woman in the back.

"Do you have a question mam?"

"Yes Major," she said. "What can you tell me about your regiment?"

"We are a reserve regiment based out of Southern Alberta," Rick said. "From time to time we are asked to contribute our people for active duty. This was such an occasion."

He sat down and pointed next to a CNN person.

"Whose idea was the broadcast of the music and the reasoning behind it."

"We felt we needed a little physiological advantage," Rick said. "Captain Hassman suggested the music. They couldn't see us, but they could hear us all around them."

"Why those choices of music," was the next question.

"Our regiment has gone to battle singing that first song since its inception. It is the first thing we are taught, is sung at every function we have and we can sing it in our sleep. The second one was mine. I kind of like Led Zeppelin, don't you? It kind of fit the situation. We do after all come from the land of ice and snow."

That comment got more than a few laughs.

"Now if you don't mind, it has been a long day and in General Khan and Major Helenchuks case a long couple of days. Perhaps a question from any members of the Ukrainian or German nations?"

A blond woman stood. "Can you explain the significance of your regimental colours," she asked in German accented English.

"As I understand it, during the early nineteenth century our regiment emigrated enmass to what was then Western Russia. That is where the eagle comes from. We were adopted into a Don Cossack Host. That is where the blue yellow red comes from. In time we had a large number of Russian born members, so the bear was introduced and of course the maple leaf represents Canada our new home."

"What then, is the significance of that?" she asked pointing above Ricks head.

He looked behind him and saw the old faded ensign was to his left and the new to his right, attached to the wall with their flag staffs crossed in the middle.

"I will answer that Major," Bashir said. "In the year 1870, my people were being subjected, as we are today, by armed Islamic Fundamentalist raiders. These raiders aim was to conquer and kill not, as they claim, to convert the unworthy, but to get rid of us. We are followers of the Prophet Mohammad after all. That year a young man, a great leader with much wisdom, came from Russia to help us with two thousand of his people. Men and women among them, all armed and trained to fight. He could speak four languages. German they spoke among themselves, Russian, French and English. The English had a small detachment of infantry and a detachment of German cavalry. In a short time, the young Russian had taken command and had established patrols of the countryside, stopping many raids and gaining the admiration of my people and our respect. His wife established a hospital and cured many of my people's ailments. His people were deeply religious, but Catholics. He answered our more radical peoples attacks by saying we all worshipped the same God, only had different profits. He had studied the Holy Koran and could answer their questions with direct quotations from it. He respected our religion and made no mention of who was right or who was wrong.

"Using the Holy Koran as a teaching tool, he taught us to respect and revere our women, to as he had, include them in every aspect of life. He taught us that he hated war and fighting, but realized that sometimes we had to fight and kill to save our people. He taught us new techniques for farming and that education of the young, all the young, male and female alike, was the key to any people's success long term. They were great horseman and horse breeders and they taught us their secrets. To this day we revere he and his people for their generosity and wisdom.

"Then one day, he received word of a great army approaching. They were ten thousand strong and they meant to destroy this man, his and my people. The enemy had learned to fear his grey uniformed troopers and their repeating rifles, so just like today, this great man dressed his men in red jackets taken from the British and lined one thousand of them in two lines blocking this very valley. The enemy, all cavalry, accepted the challenge and charged ten thousand strong against his twin line of a thousand. He opened fire at two hundred meters and kept firing. Then he was joined by those of us stationed on each flank with our older single shot rifles and we killed them all. Like today we had minimal losses and the enemy lost all.

"That great man's name was Andreas Bekenbaum and Major Richard Bekenbaum is his direct descendant. That is the meaning of the crossed flags. The reunion of the old and the new."

With that and while the press was still digesting what they had just heard, the military people stood and left the room, Bashir escorting them to another room.

"That story is to impossible to be true general," the American general said.

"No sir," Rick said. "Andreas was knighted for it by both the English and the Russians. He and indeed the whole regiment received the highest awards the Russians could give them. It is noted in our regimental history and the British as well. You can research it if you wish.

"Now if you will excuse me, Major Helenchuk has asked me if I can establish communications with her people back home and I have agreed to help."

He motioned for Tanya to proceed him and the second they were out of sight, he pulled her to him and kissed her. At first she made a week attempt to resist, placing both her palms on his chest, but in seconds she had pressed herself to him and had her hand behind his head.

"I thought I had lost you forever," he said when they broke free.

"Da, me as well," she said in Ukrainian. "You are of Andreas Host?"

"Yes you could say that," Rick said.

"Your grandfather's name is Nicolas? I met him while I was on leave back home last month," she said. "We had a big celebration of reunification. For you see, I am Andreas Host as well."

"You are the eldest in your family?" Rick asked.

"I am an only child," she said. "My father is the leader of our branch of the host."

"Well that settles it then," Rick said. "Now you have no choice but to marry me."

"But first you must ask my father and I must be approved of by your mother," Tanya said. "And before all that, I really must report home and tell them what has happened here."

"Yes of course," Rick said breaking free of her. "I am sorry, I forget myself."

"After I make my report," she said, in a husky Ukrainian accented English as she came close to him and wrapped her arms around him. "After that we can practice for the wedding night yes?" and she drew his head down to hers and kissed him, placing his hand on her breast.

"But after the report," she said breathlessly pushing him away from her and straightening her blouse. "Not now." She walked away from him swaying her hips and stopped at the outside exit, looked back at him and flicked her head so that her hair swirled around her. Then she crooked her finger at him and darted out the door with an un-officer like giggle.

Once again an uninjured Kahlil had assumed his position as Ricks batman. He entered Rick's tent without knocking and figuring out who's intertwined feet were who's stuck out from the blankets on the army cot, he kicked the bottom of Rick's hard.

"What?" Rick said. His voice cracking with sleep and more than a little hint of crankiness.

"The Majors presence are required at the landing zone," Kahlil said. "You are to greet the arriving dignitaries."

"Ah shit, it never rains but it pours," Rick said. He leaned over and gently kissed the now awake Tanya. "You even look good first thing in the morning," he said. "You might as well stay here, no sense both of us ruining our day."

"No sir," Kahlil said. "Both Majors are to be present sir, not just you, but Major Helenchuk as well."

"What?" she said in Ukrainian. "Shit!" she said in English as she started hunting for her clothing.

"Ok Kahlil, leave us now, so that the Major can keep some of her dignity," Rick said.

First Tanya punched him, then she drew him down to her. "I believe I will accept," she said.

"Accept what?" Rick asked.

"You asked me to marry you yesterday and I accept today," she said.

"It took you all night to figure that out?" Rick said.

"Not all night," she said. "But you know, you never buy a horse until after you ride it. You ride good."

She flipped him over and proved it.

It was a large contingent that exited the fleet of helicopters that landed. Members of the third battalion PPCLI took over from the Regiments people and there were replacements for the German, Ukrainians and Marines as well. Duffle bags were handed to the Marines and Germans as well as the Ukrainians and ten coffins were unloaded from one of the choppers. Bill saw that and took charge, sending some G-wagons and the HUMV truck with troopers to collect them and transport them to the hospital complex. While that was going on, the General and his staff, in dress blues descended and were joined by the families of the fallen, all of them in uniform as well, even the youngest who were Sandy's children. Bill hollered assembly and the Regiment stopped what they were doing and sprinted to form up behind Rick and Tanya. The last to depart the chopper were the colour party and they unfurled the regimental and national battle flags to let them run free in the wind. The regiment's yellow battle honours streaming away from the colour in the wind.

"COMPNAY, STAND TO ATTENTION!" Rick belted. "COMPNAY, PRESENT, HARMS!"

As one, the company snapped their hands to their foreheads as the general and the colours approached and held them there while the colour party and the grievers arranged themselves in front of the company.

"BATTALION, ATTEN-TION!" the general barked. "BATTAL-ION, SALUTE!" The regimental colours dipped and the general's party snapped their hands to their foreheads in a return salute. Both Rick's and the generals troopers snapped their hands back to their sides.

A major from the PPCLI marched stiffly in front of Rick and saluted.

"BATTALION, PREPARE TO BE RELIEVED," the general belted out.

"Major, I relieve you," the PPCLI Major said.

"Major, I stand relieved," Rick said.

"Master Warrant, the field is yours sir," Rick said.

"CHARLEY COMPNAY!" Bill yelled. "CHARLEY COMP-NAY WILL FORM AT THE REAR OF THE REGIMENT. CHARLEY COMPNAY RIGHT FACE, FORWARD MARCH!"

Bill lead them around, marching in the arm swinging Canadian march, in a series of turns until the company, still in two lines were marching in place behind the rest of the regiment.

"COMPNAY HALT. COMPNAY RIGHT FACE. AT EASE!"

Bill then marched smartly around the edge of the formation and across the front until he was opposite the general and then stopped, spun so he was facing the general and saluted.

"Charley Company all present or accounted for and in formation, sir!"

"Very well Master Warrant. Take us from the field if you please." The general said.

"BATTALION, ATTENTION!" Bill yelled. "BATTALION WILL RETIRE FROM THE FIELD IN COMPANY ORDER. BATTALION, RIGHT FACE. FORWARD MARCH!"

With Bill beside the general and followed by the regiments colonels, the colour party marched off, followed by the double line of mourners in their dress blue and Charley Company with Tanya and Rick at their head, in the desert camouflage bringing up the rear.

All of this was captured on camera and was sent around the world from the hastily set up generator powered satellite transmitters CNN had brought on site.

Once the regiment was out of site inside the walls, they were dismissed. And Charley Company dispersed taking the new comers with them. Rick went to the parents of each of the fallen troopers and shook their hands. He did well until he came to Sandy's husband and kids and he broke down and pulled the kids to his breast kissing the tops of their heads.

"I'm so sorry Hans." Rick said. "It's all my fault. The son of bitch was playing dead and before we spotted him, he launched an RPG from almost point blank range. I should have spotted it."

"So should have Sandy," Hans said. "I've been there Rick, I know and this was a much bigger action. There is no way you could possibly have seen everything. Were you with her?"

"Ya, I was holding her head." Rick said. "First she said, 'God that was fun, we sure showed those assholes not to fuck with us.'"

"Yup, that's Sandy." Hans said.

"'You tell that lunk of a husband of mine that I miss him and love him dearly and my kids that I love them and mommy will be with them always. I want to be buried beside my great great great grandmother.'"

"So she will," Hans said tears flowing down his cheeks. "Was she in much pain?"

"No, I gave her my shot first, then Harold gave her his. When she was ready, she gave me hers and helped me give it her."

"Good, thank you brother," Hans said and kissed him on the top of his head.

"The others?"

"Two of them caught the main blast, one the secondary and one died as we pulled her out of the wreck. Sandy was blown clear, but it was over in minutes Hans. She was messed up pretty good inside."

"You did the right thing. Can the kids see her?"

"Ya, she looks ok."

"Ok, thanks."

"Bill, take Hans, the kids and Sandy's folks to see her please."

"Richard, are you ok?" Emily asked him as she folded him into her arms.

"Ya, I'll be fine mom," he said kissing her on the cheek. "It was just hard telling Hans and the kids what she asked me to tell them."

"Ok Rick," Paul said. "We brought your dress uniforms and we have scheduled the funerals for three hours from now. The Ukrainians will be buried with her and Bashir's people are preparing the graves. Go get cleaned up and changed, we can talk later. Your mother will handle the press. Oh by the way, all of the Ukrainians are Andreas Host. I guess the descendants that stayed behind. I just found out on the way over here. Have you met their commander yet?"

"Ah ya," Rick said. "Remember the cute blond I danced with at the graduation party?"

"Are you kidding me!" Elizabeth said. "Christ, she had the hots for you!"

"Um, ya, I guess," Rick said.

"Good," Paul said. "You have established good relations with her, we are merging the hosts."

"Um, ya, you could say so," Rick said blushing and ducking his head.

"Richard! You didn't!" Emily said punching him on the arm.

"It runs in the genes mom," Elizabeth said, grabbing Rick and kissing him. "Just like Andreas, rescuing the damsel in distress."

"Oh now I get it," Paul said.

"Oh Gees dad!" Elizabeth said. "Was he always this dense mom?"

"Yes, I believe he was, why I remember..."

Rick took this as his cue and took off at a run for his tent.

"Ok people," Bill said to the assembled charley company now in their blue dress uniforms. "First we will escort the four who are going home, taking Sandy with us. Once they are placed on the choppers, we will escort Sandy to her resting spot, we will be joined by the Ukrainian delegation at that point. After the funeral, General Kahn's people have planned a reception for us. Our fallen brothers and sister will be transported to Kandahar airport and will be waiting for us there. Half of you and the mourners will accompany them home. The other half will accompany the Ukrainians home. They have a ceremony planned for us there. We will work out who goes where later. If you really want either, let me know, otherwise we will just pick names at random. Questions?"

"Can we come back?" Al asked. "I really feel I have to finish my tour, that I owe it to Sandy and the others."

The rest of the company indicated the same.

"I will bring it up with the general," Rick said. "I can't promise anything though, but I would like to do the same."

"Hey Gadget, maybe you could convince that hot Ukrainian major to join us," Al said. "Maybe on an exchange program?"

"Hey, you're already taken you dope," Julia said. "Besides, I have it on good authority that Gadget and Hotty are a number."

"Ah, say it aint so Gadget," Al pleaded. "Damn, maybe she has some cute buddies."

"I'll cute buddy you, shit head!" Julia said punching Al in the arm.

"See what happens when you get hooked up with a hottie Gadget," Al said. "Run while you still can."

Al and Julia had been married before the company had deployed.

"Ok, ok enough," Rick said as the fun threatened to get out of control.

"The press will be following our every move. Not one hair out of place people. Not one unaccounted movement or gesture, is that clear. Sandy deserves our best and you will damn well give it to her!"

"Take us out Master Warrant."

They marched out, berets squared away instead of the raked back style they usually wore. When they reached where the bodies were kept, the forty troopers, chosen by lot to be the pawl bearers, marched in, while the rest of the company formed up to each side of the door. They were placed at ease while they waited. Then Bill had them come to attention and perform the rifle salute as the Maple Leaf flag draped coffins were one by one marched out between the lines. Then they faced front and marched alongside the coffins, weapons on shoulders until they reached the Chinook that would take the coffins to Kandahar. Sandy was placed so her coffin oversaw the proceedings and one by one the coffins were loaded into the Chinook.

Taking a glance around, Rick saw that Whitmore and the Germans had joined up on the edges of the Regiment in their own dress uniforms, with National and regimental flags flying at their fore. Rick about faced and quick marched to his father, came to attention and saluted.

"Permission to speak," he said quietly and his father nodded.

"General, it is only fitting that all the members of Bravo Task Force be represented in the party sir."

"Make it so," his father said.

Rick saluted and approached the Marines first.

"Captain, if you would honour us by joining our parade and if one of your troops could volunteer as a pawl bearer, it would be an honour sir."

"Sar, with your permission sar, the Gunnery Sergeant would volunteer sar!"

"Aye aye Gunnery Sergeant, permission granted. It would be our pleasure Major to join your honour guard."

"Gunnery Sergeant, you will accompany me. Captain have your people join the guard on the right if you please."

"Aye Aye major."

Rick then marched down the front of the formation, the gunnery sergeant two steps behind him, while the other Marines joined up with the honour guard, except the colour party which placed itself behind and to the side of the Canadians colour party.

"Captain," Rick said in German to Erich. "It would be an honour, if you would join our honour party sir and if one of your troopers would volunteer to join us as a pawl bearer."

"Sir, the Senior Sergeant will volunteer sir!" and he strode forward to join the Gunnery Sergeant.

"Very well Captain, have your people join the honour guard on the left if you will."

Again as Rick marched the two sergeants across the front of the column, the Germans joined the honour party to the left and the German colour party joined the main body to the rear and left of the Canadian colours.

"Master Warrant," Rick said. "The Senior Sergeant and the Gunnery Sergeant will help bear the Captain."

"Sir, yes sir." Bill said. "Gentlemen, it is not far and level. We will be slow marching, try and match our gate if you please. Hand your rifles and head gear to the sergeant here. You will get them back after you place the coffin. You are pretty much the same size as my people so we will slot you in the second row ok?"

Patricia took the weapons and head gear and placed them into the spotless LAV that would be trailing them and rejoined the company.

"We are ready anytime you are Major," Bill said.

"Right. Master Warrant take us out," Rick said.

The commands were given in hushed tones and the colour parties joined the head of the procession, the Regiment and other dignitaries joining the rear after saluting the flag draped coffin as it passed and behind the LAV. No words were spoken, the Regiment forming in column of four, the only sound, the sound of boots hitting the ground in slow unified precision. The LAV halted and the four Ukrainian flag draped coffins and honour guard joined the procession, the honour guard marching in the high leg, arm across chest fashion of the earlier Soviet era. A BMP armoured vehicle joined beside the LAV and the Ukrainian delegation joined to the left of the Canadian, also in column of four. The only difference in uniform was the Ukrainian flag on the shoulder instead of the maple leaf, the lack of bears, eagles and crossed rifles on the collars, the rank insignias and they wore lamb skin head gear.

Rick saw it as it came into view. A well-kept and maintained grave yard and they went to the open graves that were in a roped off area in the centre. The three existing graves were immaculate. They had carved stones around the edges and the head stones were clean and clearly legible. Sandy was placed beside her ancestor and the Ukrainian troopers beside the other two graves, two to a side. The colour parties arranged themselves in front and the troops formed up behind them. Rifles and head gear given back to the bearers who rejoined the honour guards.

The Regiments priest strode forward and began to conduct the sermon. He split it between English and Ukrainian and all to soon was finished. The regimental bugler marched forward and the soul wrenching last post was played, the colours dipping until they almost touched the ground.

When he was done, the honour guard fired a company salute. Each rifle firing when the trooper heard the rifle next to him discharge. Then rifles grounded, the Canadian honour guard began to sing softly. The song was picked up immediately by the Ukrainian honour guard and the two groups sang the first verse and refrain alone. The pawl bearers grabbed waiting shovels and began filling the graves. When the second verse started, the rest of the Regiment and the Ukrainians joined, singing the next verse and refrain softly and in harmony with each other. The graves were filled quickly. Then each verse after, increased in tempo and volume and went from a slow mournful sound, to a fast joyous one. And without a spoken command, the colours jumped up ward and the assembled troops quick marched out of the grave yard, pushing their hats off of their foreheads and back to the rear of their heads.

The song and the march abruptly ended where Bashir and his people were waiting. The tables were piled high with food and bottles of vodka and the party started.

Rick was seated with his parents and sister and while he kept up his end of the conversation, his mind was elsewhere, scanning the crowd for Tanya. He spotted her once in a while, but she was also kept busy and his glimpses were fleeting and rare.

Finally after one of his sisters jokes at his expense and she kissing him on the cheek afterward. He excused himself and went to the area set up as a latrine. Tanya was waiting for him when he left. Her hands on her hips and not exactly pleased.

"So, My Lord, the great Major Bekenbaum throws me aside the first chance he gets when his Canadian girlfriend arrives!" she burst out in Ukrainian.

"Woa up there Tanya it's not like that at all!" Rick said, raising both his hands to shoulder height palms forward. "She was just pissing with me getting me all riled up. You saw I left as soon as I could. I've been looking for a chance to ditch them all night."

"Really?" Tanya said letting her hands drop to her side. "You are not lying to me? I would understand. She is very beautiful and from your homeland."

"Did I not ask you to marry me? Did I not promise to ask your father for your hand? That was not and is not lie. I love you Tanya, God help me but I do."

She came up to him then shyly, her eyes down cast and she played with his tie as she spoke.

"And I love you," she said in English. "God help me too."

He tilted her head up by the chin and brushed her hair back so he could see her eyes and kissed her.

"Well come on then," he said. "The general has asked to meet you."

"And then I can meet your parents?" she asked.

"Um sure, why not, I guess so," Rick said.

"Oh you men. Always so scared." Tanya said. "I am sure your parents are fine people."

"Ya, I guess you could say that, sure."

"Oh come on, it can't be that bad!" she said, holding his left arm in both of hers as they came up to the generals table, she dropped them and came to attention.

The General and the colonels rose to greet them.

"General, Colonels, may I present Major Tanya Helenchuk. Major Helenchuk, may I present my parents, General Paul Bekenbaum, my mother Colonel Emily Bekenbaum and my sister, Colonel Elizabeth Von Hoaedle."

"Oh what a pleasure to meet you again!" Elizabeth said. "We had the pleasure of dancing with you at the graduation ceremony!"

Tanya spun on him and pointed her finger at him.

"Hey, I tried to tell you." Rick said raising his hands again.

"Tell her what dear?" Emily said. "A pleasure to meet you Tanya. Rick has told us so little about you."

"Oh come on mom," Elizabeth said. "I could tell at the grad party he had the hots for her. Christ he mopped about for a month after she left."

"You did what?" Tanya said spinning back to glare at him.

"Mopped dear," Emily said. "He wouldn't eat, was cranky and hard to get along with. You know, mopped."

"Yes, much like Tanya did when she got home," a Ukrainian accented voice said from behind Rick. "Mama thought sure she had caught some dreadful Canadian disease."

"Sergei you old reprobate," Paul said. "How the hell are you? Sonya, so good to see you again. Emily you remember Sergei and Sonya?"

"How could I not?" Emily said. "We shared the same dugout for two nights in Bosnia."

"You what?" Rick said.

"Hey, we weren't always old and grey you know." Paul said. "We had our share of bullets pass over our heads."

"Colonel, Captain, may I present Major Richard Bekenbaum. Major, my parents, Colonel Sergei Helenchuk and Captain Sonya Halenchuk."

Rick shook her father's hand and her mother grabbed him and kissed him on both cheeks. She held him at arm's length and looked him over.

"Tanya, you better grab hold of this one," she said in Ukrainian. "He's a keeper."

"Isn't he just," Elizabeth said, also in Ukrainian. "I am Elizabeth, Rick's sister."

Another round of handshakes and hugs and kisses later and Elizabeth said. "You know, both of these idiots need to be told they love each other."

"Liz!" Rick said.

"Colonel Liz to you little brother," she said, sticking her tongue out at him. She grabbed Tanya's hand and dragged her to ladies room.

"When I saw you at the dance," Tanya said. "I thought you and Sandy were after him. You both were so beautiful and gracious and he so handsome. Then he played coy and for the first time in my life I had to work for a man. God how I hated you both. Then he chose me and I thought I would die. Then I ran before I lost control of myself."

She stopped talking and held Elisabeth's hand as she looked out across the field.

"Then life returned to normal and I was stationed here. These people are so wonderful, generous, giving. Then the Taliban hit us and I found out how fierce they were. We kept fighting and Bashir gave me a head set radio and I jury rigged an antennae for it and called and called and finally a voice in Russian answered. He was so calm, so reassuring. He told me to hang on, that they were coming. He gave me a new frequency to tune to and later that night Bashir talked to him and a smile came to his face and he said to me 'Now we are safe, God has answered our prayers.'"

She stopped again and Elizabeth let her be, knowing she was reliving the moment.

"We lined the battlements with all the weapons and bullets we had left. The voice had told us to wait for his signal that he would be here. But we did not know when and the Taliban were massing and then a sound from heaven came. It came from all around us and above us and it was his voice. 'When you fuck with friends of the regiment,' he said in English, 'you fuck with us.' Then he switched to Russian and gave his oath to Bashir and the music started. Our music. Faster and faster it came, many voices joining in. I and my comrades too, we sang and sang and at the climax, explosions ran through the Taliban as the drones fired their rockets at the mortar and RPG positions. They raked them with passes from the mini guns at the end of the song. Then a Rock and Roll song started and at the words 'We come from the land of ice and snow' the LAVs broke the crest of the hill, battle flags flying and guns blazing and the whole hill side on both sides erupted in fire. Then came the HUMVs and G-Wagons from the south and the Taliban had nowhere to run, nowhere to hide and we fired everything we had and the Taliban died where they stood. When it was over we cheered and cheered and the troops came down from the hills and celebrated the great victory. My comrades and I rushed out the gate to join the celebration and were almost there when the Taliban pointed the RPG at Sandy's LAV and fired. Rick saw it out the corner of his eye and swung his machine gun and fired, but to late."

She paused again looking with blank eyes into the field. Then she took Elizabeth's hand.

"We ran to help and God help me, I saw it was him and I saw he held Sandy's head in his lap and was stroking her hair. She saw me and smiled. 'Gadget she said, you better grab hold of that girl and never let her go. She loves you like crazy.' And she died. He was crying as he laid her down and stood and turned and looked at me. God I wanted to hug him so! He nodded to me and started yelling orders and I thought he had lost interest, so collected my people and began to help with the wounded. At the celebration party he found me and told me he loved me."

Elizabeth waited for a moment and couldn't stand it anymore. "And?" she asked.

"Well a girl doesn't buy a horse without riding it first," Tanya said smiling.

"And?" Elizabeth said.

"I think I'll keep him," Tanya said before Elizabeth bear hugged her.

"But my father must approve, as must your mother," Tanya said.

"Wait here," Elizabeth said. "Don't move." And she sprinted away back to the party, dragging her mother back a short time later.

"Ok Liz I'm here, what's all this about?" she said somewhat perturbed.

"Colonel, I, I mean Mrs. Bekenbaum," Tanya began. "I would, with your permission, marry your son Richard. I do not have much. I have enough money saved up to start a house hold and have five cows and four horses of my own. I am an only child and will inherit my father's holdings in time. We are not rich, but the land is good and I can rent it out easily."

"Hmm," Emily said not committing. "What of my son then? Do you love him then?"

"Oh yes mam, with all my heart and all my soul, so help me God," Tanya said becoming frantic. "I promise not to be a burden mam. I will work hard. I know your son does not have much, but what is mine will be his."

"When I met Richards's father he was not even a Master Warrant, only a lowly Warrant. He said he was only a poor farmer and had a few horses. But God how I loved him." Emily said. She starred into the distance for a while.

"My family was rich and somewhat powerful and my mother did not approve and forbid me to marry or even to be with him. My father over ruled her and then we met Tatiana, Paul's grandmother and his grandfather John. In a short period of time my mother was on board."

"If my son loves you as much as I can see you love him, you have my blessing daughter."

"What did that jerk of a brother of mine tell you about himself?" Elizabeth said.

"Not that much. I know he was a Master Warrant and that he just recently was made a Major. Mostly because of politics he said. He said he is a poor farmer and owns a few horses and cattle and dabbles a little with electrons as a hobby. He's not sure how much money he has, but says it is not much. Don't worry Elizabeth, I have enough, we won't suffer."

"My dear," Emily said. "My son owns about a thousand head of cattle and at last count, over a hundred of our best horses. He and his partners own all the patents and manufacturing rights to all the drones everyone is using. He has enough money of his own never to have to work another day of his or his grandchildren's lives. That's not including his share of the family trust and the money he receives from the Earldom. He has over one thousand square miles of deeded land he oversees in Canada and is your landlord in Ukraine. When it is time he will be Ataman of Andreas Host. He is a poor farmer alright. Just as his father was.

"Come my daughters it is to cold out here for me and I want to dance."

The three of them, Tanya in the middle, Emily to the right and Elizabeth to the left, came back, arms wrapped around each other and as they reached the edge of the celebration, Emily began to sing in Russian. Elizabeth and Tanya joined in and they began to dance as they came closer to the dance floor. Sonya saw what was going on and broke in beside her daughter and the two mothers together with Tanya in the centre made their way to the dance floor while Elizabeth danced to Rick and pulled him to the floor to join them. The Ukrainian women broke from husbands and friends and joined, making a circle around Rick and Tanya who were left alone in the centre. Then Julia, Patricia and the other women from the regiment joined, their voices joined in harmony.

Suddenly they stopped dancing and singing and started a new song, slowly. Tanya spread her arms and began to dance slowly around Rick. Coming close, then scampering back out of his reach when he reached for her. Now the men joined the circle and joined the song and Rick strode away from Tanya ignoring her and started his own dance, swirling and prancing. First approaching Julia, then dancing away to Patricia, then to a striking Ukrainian woman, then to Elizabeth, then to Sonya. Tanya made to grab his arm and he spun away from her to the other side of the circle and stood with his hands on his hips and his head held high as he looked at her.

The men stopped singing and the women began again and Tanya began a slow dance she swung her hips first this way, then that. Arched her back and turned to the side, all the while coming closer to Rick until she was within his reach and she stopped, her legs crossed at the ankles, her hands by her side and her head and eyes down cast.

Rick took his hands from his hips and crossed his arms on his chest. The men began to sing softly as Rick walked slowly around Tanya looking her up and down, until he was in front of her. Then he reached his right hand out to her and she extended her left until their fingers were touching and they turned side by side and began a slow dance in step and the women joined the men and the song sang soft and slow, then began to rise in tempo and sound and the two dancers matched the tempo until finally it was fast and they were facing each other and Rick tossed her into the air and caught her again and she fell into his arms and he swung her around, her long blond hair flying free and he spun her around and pulled her close and they kissed. And they kissed and they kissed. And the crowd cheered.

Rick and Tanya broke the kiss and arm and arm returned to their seats and were soon joined by their parents and Elizabeth.

"Paul dear," Emily said. "Why don't we, Sergei and Sonya and the children go for a walk?"

The two families left the celebration and walked to where Elizabeth and Tanya had been earlier.

"Well?" Emily said looking at Rick.

"Well what?" Rick asked and he was kicked in the shin by Elizabeth.

"Shit Liz, that hurt," he said. "Really, well what?" he asked again this time being kicked by Tanya.

"Are you that dense boy?" Paul said.

Rick looked at Tanya, who shot a glance at her father and put her hands together in a sign of prayer and mouthed please to him. Rick took a deep swallow and walked up to Tanya's father.

"Mr. Halenchuk. I would like to marry your daughter. I am in good health and have a good job and can support her and our children when the time comes. What little I have will be hers and I promise to treat her well always. May I have your blessing sir?"

"Do you love her?" he asked.

"Yes sir, I do."

"That is a bonus," he said and grunted as his wife kicked him. He looked at her and she nodded. Then looked at Emily and she nodded.

"You have my blessing," he said. "If she will have you."

Rick took a sigh of relief and walked back to Tanya, "Well that's that then" he said, putting his arm around her. She slapped it away and stepped back from him.

"What now?" Rick asked and before his mother could punch him, he walked up to Tanya, went to one knee in front of her and took her right hand in both of his.

"Tanya Helenchuk, I love you more than I love life. Would you marry me?"

She dropped to her knees. "Yes you big dummy. Yes."

As she kissed him, camera flashes went off all around them from cameras and cell phones and a great cheer rang out.

"Shit, is nothing a secret around here?" Rick asked.

"Al told you to run you big dummy," Julia said and she kissed first Rick and then Tanya. Followed by Patricia and all the rest of Charley Company including the Americans and the Germans. Then all of Tanya's company and then the party was really on.

Tanya awoke. Her eyes looked at the wall of a tent and it took her a moment to realize where she was. She was laying on her stomach and was naked. The tent was warm, but not hot yet and the covers were down to her butt. Feeling the warm body beside her, she turned her head and saw the bare shoulder beside her. It was a strong muscular arm and above that were good chest muscles with light almost invisible hair. She looked further up and right into pale blue eyes that were looking at her and she felt herself being pulled into them. He was laying on his side with his head propped up with his hand and he was smiling. He brushed her hair out of her eyes and then her spine tingled as he gently ran a finger down it and back up again. She turned so that she was facing him and wrapped a leg around his.

"Good morning beautiful," he said.

"As if," she said and she ran her hand down his arm. He had a small scar across one shoulder and she ran a finger along it.

Rick felt the electricity from her touch along the scar and shivered. She smiled and her face came alive. The yellow flecks around the irises of her green eyes caught the light and sparkled and he gently brushed her long blond hair with a finger down and away from a perfect breast and circled her nipple with his finger. Her hand strayed to his stomach and gently rubbed his abs and then she too circled her finger around his nipple and he smiled. Life was good he thought.

"Where did you get that?" she asked stroking his scar once again.

"Not sure," Rick said. "Chad maybe? Forgot to duck. It was no big deal."

"Are you on active duty a lot?"

"Ya. I like to keep busy," Rick said. "Lately it's been a lot of training. I'm kind of in an anti-insurgent group. This was the first time in a couple of years that the whole company has been together. How about you?"

"It has mostly been training and administration duties for me," Tanya said. "Like that liaison job I had when we first met. God the arrogance of that Navy Commander. It still makes me angry to think of it. This was my first field assignment. I am a communications specialist and was getting the site ready for you people when all this happened. Why do they call you Gadget?"

"I've been called that since I was about twelve," Rick said. "There was a cartoon character on TV called Inspector Gadget. He was always coming up with new inventions. I liked taking things apart and seeing what made them work. Sometimes I made them work better, that's how Harold and I became friends. Well we were on the football team together too. Both of us were kind of outcasts because we weren't chasing girls and partying all the time like the other guys. He was experimenting with a wing design for a model aircraft but the engine he had was a little week, so I took it apart and made it better and we went from there.

"They called us the Geek Squad after that. We wanted a little more range, so we tinkered with the radio system and got it to work better and then we thought it would be kind of cool, so we installed a miniature camera on board and started playing around more with the electronics and fitted the motherboard from a netbook computer in it and got GPS telemetry working. Harold kept modifying the wing and fuselage design and I kept playing with the engine designs and soon we were flying the thing a hundred kilometres away. We still had some problems with control and software issues though. Our football team won our division and I was to get an award and had to have a date for the award dance and I took a chance and asked Sandy. She was the head cheerleader and the most popular girl in school, so I thought my chances were pretty slim, but she said yes. But it didn't work out. When we kissed it was like kissing my sister and she thought the same way. Anyway, it turns out she was a computer whiz and I convinced her to come and take a look at our stuff and she spotted the software glitch right away and fixed it. After that, she, Harold and I were hardly ever apart. We went through basic together and were assigned to the same platoon."

"So not just a hunky pretty face, but you have something in there as well," Tanya said, poking her finger at the side of his temple. "Strong, handsome, smart and rich. I got the whole package."

"I suppose so," Rick said. "But I got beautiful, smart and rich as well."

"I?" Tanya said. "I am not rich. Nor am I beautiful. It is only the makeup."

"You didn't have any on after the fight," Rick said. "You were dirty, had gunpowder stains on your face and your hair was poking out all over the place. And you were the most beautiful thing I had seen in my life. As for rich. You are rich in what really matters."

Rick put his hand on her chest between her breasts. "You are rich in heart and in soul. Rich in places that money can't buy and I love you."

She pulled him to her and kissed him. Then looked back at him.

"Oh God!" She said. "What time is it? We have to see off our parents and we have to leave ourselves. Shit, where are my clothes? I need to change uniforms. Shit, shit shit."

"Excuse us Majors?" Kahlil said from outside the tent. "May we enter?"

Rick bounced off the cot and pulled on his pants and Tanya pulled the covers up to her chin.

"Ya sure, come on in," Rick said.

Rick had jammed his feet into his socks and combat boots and was standing buttoning his shirt up when the tent flap was held open. Tanya saw a tall striking Afghan woman duck her head and enter, coming to attention at the foot of the cot and holding Tanya's desert camouflage uniform on a hanger in one hand and a small garment bag in the other. Her dark blond hair was tucked under her uniform cap, she had lieutenant's insignia on her impeccable tunic and a pistol strapped to her waist. She held her head level and her dark blue eyes focused at the top corner of the bed. Kahlil entered holding a tray with a pot of coffee, two cups and a bottle of vodka on it. He also was in uniform and had a pistol strapped on.

"Fatima!" Rick said. "So good to see you again. I see you have passed your exams, congratulations. Your father must be proud."

"Thank you Major," Fatima said. "It is good to see you again as well." She was talking with an English accent.

"Yes, yes," Kahlil said. "Enough of this chit chat. This is compliments of Colonel Liz. She said something about the hair of the dog. Sub Lieutenant Kahn has been assigned as the Majors aide until the Major leaves Kabul."

Rick had finished buckling on his pistol belt, pulled out the old ACP Colt, checked the magazine and safety and placed it back into his holster. Then he grabbed his C7, made sure he had a full clip in place and that the chamber was empty and hung the strap on his left shoulder.

"Just straight coffee for me," Rick said. "Outside if you will Kahlil. Leave the tray and we'll give the Major some privacy eh?"

"Hey Bill," Rick said as he came out of the tent and sat down at the table in front of it. He took a swig of coffee and bent over to tie up his boot laces.

"We are all ship shape and ready to go," Bill said. "The Marines, Germans and Ukrainians are set and a resupply convoy of Bashir's people will be coming along. We rounded up enough ammo from the Taliban to equip the Ukrainians and the Afghanis. We are just waiting to break down your tent and we are good to go."

"Ok, send out the scouts," Rick said. "What do you figure? Three days?"

"Scouts are already gone. Day and a half tops," Bill said. "We have been guaranteed air cover the whole way and can be out of bad guy country by noon. If there are any bad guys left that is. Good morning Major."

"Good morning Master Warrant," Tanya said, tucking a stray strand of hair under her cap.

Fatima had the dress uniform on the hanger now and walked away with it.

"Your people are formed up with us already Major," Bill said. "We are just waiting on sleepy head here to get his butt in gear and we can take off."

Kahlil started issuing orders to a small army of Afghan troopers and they soon had Rick's gear and tent squared away and loaded on his nearby LAV.

Rick and Tanya walked hand in hand to her BMP. Her troopers all gathered around it.

"Well I guess this is it until tonight then," Rick said.

"I miss you already," she said. She looked around at all the staring faces.

"Fuck it," she said and grabbed the back of Ricks head, folded herself into him and kissed him.

Her troopers cheered and whistled and Rick patted her rear as she climbed aboard the BMP and then he and Bill walked back to his LAV.

"How come you never do that with me anymore?" Bill called up to Patricia in her driver's compartment.

"Oh it is unseemly for the mere sergeant to throw herself at the mighty Master Warrant in public anymore." She said.

Bill climbed upon the bow, bent down and kissed her.

"That's more like it," she said in a husky voice. "See you later. You take care now, you here?"

"Crap, the neighbourhood has gone all to shit," Al yelled over from the top of his LAV. "How do you transfer out of this Hippy love troop."

"I'll hippy love you tonight you jerk," Julia said. "Just wait till I get a hold of you."

"Crank it up Pat," Rick said and he waved his hand over his head. Any retort Al had was drowned out by the sound of diesel engines firing up.

A day and a half later, they had turned their LAVs over to their replacements. Paid their final respects to the fallen as they were boarded on the transport home and were boarding an aircraft headed for an airport in Eastern Ukraine.

The next day and a half were a blur. First they were greeted at the airport and made to stand for an hour listening to dignitaries say their speeches. Then they were boarded onto busses and driven to the barracks town. After that, proceeded by Tanya's regimental colour party, with Tanya perched in the open turret of a BMP eyes fixed rigidly ahead and her troopers standing at attention in their open hatches. Rick and his half company, in desert camouflage, berets square on heads and C7's on shoulders, marched behind the BMP down the main street of the town. Both sides of the street lined with cheering crowds, welcoming home the heroes.

Then another round of standing at parade rest listening to more speeches and they were escorted to their barracks. They spent the rest of the day brushing creases out of dress uniforms, polishing buttons and boots before going exhausted to bed only to get up early the next morning. They grabbed a quick breakfast, then started over again on the uniforms, finally donning them and perfecting them again, walked down to the assembly area. He caught a quick glimpse of Tanya, her dress uniform impeccable, her hair tucked up under the lambs skin cap, before the order was given to assemble and they marched to the hockey arena where the memorial service and reception was to be held.

Rick was seated at the head table, two seats away from the centre and Tanya the same on the other side and Rick felt his mind wander as he listened to another round of speeches. He perked up when Tanya spoke drinking in her beauty as she spoke. Her hair had been braided and curled around the back of her head in the traditional style and she spoke with a firm elegance. Of the bravery of her troops. She finished and sat down and he lost sight of her once again. Then to his surprise, they called on him to speak. He rose, took his glass with him and stood, looking out at the crowd of expectant faces and searched for something to say.

"When you are a soldier, you spend days and years training and perfecting your skills. Hoping one day to be allowed to use them and praying to God you never have to. During peace time, many of us never get the chance to find out if we are good enough, would we have passed that ultimate test? Never knowing if we would have or not.

"For those of us who have been called to duty. We find that most times it is more of the same but more intense. A typical day in the field begins with a cup of barely warm instant coffee followed by a mouth full of freeze dried mush that is called food. Then if you are lucky, you are crammed into a hot, dusty, smelly armoured vehicle and bounced around for a couple of hours with nine other dusty, dirty and smelly people. If you are on foot patrol, you have a sixty pound pack on your back and you curse the heat or the rain or the snow you are marching through and the officers that ordered you to do it.

"At the end of the day, once again you have your mouthful of mush for supper and curl up under your vehicle or tarp and try to sleep on the cold ground. The next day you start all over. All the time you are vigilant, even while sleeping. You know, *you* will never be killed or hurt, but your comrade might. So you are always on the lookout for that hidden sniper or booby trap, you have to spot it before the bad guy can kill your comrade.

"In this last engagement I had two failures and those failures cost lives. First, I was a day and a half late getting to the village. If I had been on time, perhaps our fire power and presence would have prevented the enemy from attacking and your sons and brothers would be alive. The second mistake I made was after the fight. I let down my guard and five of my troopers, my friends, one of them a mother of two young children, died because of it. Both of these were my failures. Not my troops and not their commanders. Mine. I was the commander, it was my orders that were followed and it was my lack of attention to detail that got my friends killed.

"Only those of us who have been there and done that know. Know of the bonds that bind us. No matter the nation or army unit. Those of us that have been there can look into another's eyes and know instantly that the other has experienced what we have. Within our own units and troops, we form life long bonds that can never be broken. That are stronger than blood relations, or even of that of husband and wife, or child and parent. We would sacrifice ourselves in a heart beat for our comrades and they for us.

"The day of the attack, your brothers and sisters were down to their last two clips of ammunition each. When we attacked, they fixed bayonets and charged out the front gate to help us. They came to help us, we from another country, whom they had never met. That is true courage. That is true love."

Rick raised his glass over his head, then pointed it at the pictures of the fallen troopers.

"To our absent comrades," he said, drained the glass and sat down.

Tanya stood in the silence that followed and raised her glass and pointed it the portraits and waited in silence. The first to stand were Charley Company, followed quickly by Tanya's troops, then the head table rose, followed by the whole auditorium. Then Tanya brought the glass back and drained it. She stayed standing as everyone else sat and walked back to the podium motioned for her glass to be refilled and waited, her hands griping the sides of the podium and her head down until she saw all the glasses refilled then, she stood straight and held her head high.

"We have heard speeches of courage and honour and devotion to duty here tonight," she said. "It took a stranger. A stranger to our country, our community, our customs. It took a stranger to tell us the truth. The truth as to how it really is. The terror we all feel, waiting for the next gunshot or the next RPG or motor round to explode. Hoping and praying it will not be you that is hit and then feeling guilty about it later.

"All that being said, I have never witnessed such bravery, such audacity as I did that day. Charley Company came flying over that hill, flags flying and guns blazing. Both hill sides erupted in flame and noise as the infantry opened up with their rifles and machine guns. Those of us inside, knew we were saved and we rushed out, more to greet than to help, but we shot anyway. They did not need our help, but we helped anyway.

"He said he failed. He did not. People die in wars all of the time. I watched this man comfort his friend as she lay dying in his arms. I saw the tears in his eyes as he told her husband and children her last words of love for them."

She stopped then, as the emotions took hold of her and she could not speak for a moment.

"This is true courage, this is true love of a comrade. It is not something many of us can or could do, yet he did. His actions and the actions of Bravo Task Force, saved not only us. He saved thousands of Afghans who would all have been murdered had he not come. He did not fail us, he saved us."

She raised her glass and pointed it at Rick. "To Major Richard Bekenbaum, Fourth Earl of Didsbury, future Ataman of Andreas Host and future husband of Tanya, who loves him with all her heart and soul." She drained her glass and smashed it on the floor with all her might.

Two hours later, Rick felt an arm go through his and looked down to see Tanya's beaming face.

"I wonder gentlemen?" she said to Rick's conversation partners. "If I could steal my future husband for a few moments? It is so hot and smoky in here and I could use some fresh air. It is such a beautiful night tonight."

As soon as she walked out the door she steered him around a corner of the auditorium, pulled him close and kissed him.

"Oh I have missed you so these last few days," she murmured into his ear holding him tight.

"Come, it really is a beautiful night and I really do want to go for a walk in the starlight with my lover." She said pushing him gently away.

They walked for a while hand in hand, enjoying the night. I am one lucky man Rick thought looking over at her. The way the moon and starlight shined on her face was spectacular and she looked up at him at that moment and smiled and he thought the world could end right now and he would not notice.

"You gave a beautiful speech tonight Rick," she said. "No one ever talks of the things you did, but you did it so well and so clear. I wasn't your fault you know. It wasn't Whitmore's either, I checked. His Colonel wouldn't authorize him to leave. He had a problem putting his troops under your command. He has since been relieved and forced to retire."

"Good, I met him. He was a real asshole."

"In any case, even if you had been on time, my people would have still died. They hit us the day before you were to have arrived. They were hoping for a quick kill, then to ambush and wipe you out. We got that from some wounded prisoners the day before you arrived. They hadn't counted on all the fire power Bashir had."

"There is still Sandy," Rick said.

"People die in war Rick. That's what we get paid for. She knew the risks and was willing to do it, just as you and I are. She was just as much to blame as you were. She should have been watching and so should have her people. We were all caught up in the moment Rick."

"Ya, that's what Hans said too," Rick said.

"We do the best we can my love. We learn from our mistakes and we move on. I can see a number of things I could have done differently and maybe my people would not have died. But what is that saying you have? Hind sight is twenty twenty."

"How did you get to be so damn smart?" Rick said and he stopped and kissed her.

"Oh I'm not that smart," she said. "I let you catch me didn't I?" Then she pushed him away and ran.

Damn she's fast, Rick thought as he sprinted after her. She kept just out his reach, taking him off the main street to a back one. Then after a couple of blocks she began to slow, but so did he. If he came to close, she increased her speed and then she darted at the last minute into another lane that soon turned to gravel and her gate changed to that of a long distance runner, but still kept ahead of him. She made a final turn up a little used pathway. Trees spread their branches across the path and they were plunged into darkness. Her dark uniform hid her from view, but he focused on her foot falls and kept going. Shortly they broke into a clearing with a small cabin nestled in the back and rail fences lined the pathway to both sides. She sprinted that last few meters and up the three steps that led to a covered porch with a two person swing attached to the ceiling and she stopped. Putting her hands on her knees and breathing hard.

Rick joined her on the porch and turned around to survey the scene from the porch in the moonlight. Old habits dying hard, he scanned the tree line, all his senses alive, looking for intruders or hidden attackers, then remembered where he was and relaxed and took in the quiet solitude of the spot.

Oh my God, she thought. Look at him, hardly breathing hard. She had done this with others in the past and most of them had not even made it halfway, let alone kept up with her and pushed her to her limit. Finally she got her breath back and her heart slowed down enough for her to speak.

"Come sit down," she said. "That was a long run, you did well."

He just looked at her and said nothing, but smiled a little smile, picked her up and sat down putting her on his lap as he did so.

"You, my love, have been behind a desk to long," he said. "My mother can run farther than that."

"Hey, I qualify at the front every year!" she said pouting. "I beat most of the guys!"

"What's the elevation here?" he asked. "A couple of hundred meters above sea level? Where I live, it's a thousand and where we regularly train, it's almost two thousand. That's probably why."

"Oh, yes you are most likely right," she said calming down.

"This is a nice place, something like mine at home, but with more and denser trees," Rick said. "Is it ok for us to be here? Do you know the owner?"

"Yes it is ok for us to be here," Tanya said. "You could say I know the owner."

She jumped off his lap, walked to a corner of the porch, raised up on her tip toes and retrieved a key from inside the rafters. She unlocked the door and went inside, turning on a lamp and beckoning him in. It was a single room, about twenty by thirty. At the back, was a small kitchen and a partition separated a bathing and toilet area. Along one wall, was a large duvet covered double bed. The other side held a kitchen table and a small work bench. The room was definitely female and Rick heard the door shut behind him.

"Welcome to my home Richard," she said softly behind him.

Rick turned and saw she had unbuttoned her blouse down to her skirt and that she was not wearing a bra. He soon found out how soft the bed really was.

Tanya woke up to the smell of burning solder and the sight of the sun streaming into the front window. She turned over and saw Rick at her work bench, his eye to the large mounted and lighted magnifying glass she had mounted on it, soldering a component to a small circuit board. When he was done, he took her multi meter and tested the component, nodded and testing the circuit again and frowning. She admired his back muscles and then quietly walked over to the bathroom. When she came out, he was still at it and she noticed that he had found his duffle bag, she had brought over by a close friend and that he was wearing his camo pants, but was still bare chested and bare foot. While she watched him work, she found his discarded white dress shirt on the floor, brought it to her nose and took in his sent from it, before donning it, letting it hang loose on her shoulders and doing up the bottom two buttons. As she walked to him, she flipped her hair out from under the collar and let it spill down her back. She noticed the callouses on his shoulders from the straps of the sixty pound packs he wore and saw a deep and long scar along the shoulder blades and across his back. As she gingerly fingered the scar, he caught her hand and looked up at her.

"Good morning sleepy head," he said and the smile left his face as he saw the look of concern on her face. He spun around on the stool and took her head in his hands.

"What's wrong? Having second thoughts?"

"That was a bad one Rick," she said softly, her hand still on the scar at his back.

"Nah," he said smiling. "It looks worse than it was."

"I know, you forgot to duck," she said.

"No, actually I ducked when I shouldn't have and got jammed into the back of the turret. Stupid me."

He stuck his hand in the shirt and cupped a breast while he kissed her.

"While I admire the view, I think your attire hardly fitting for you to take me on a tour of your place," he said.

"Oh, you are tired of touring my body already and want to see my land?" she said pouting.

"No," he said pinching her nipple, "And yes, I want a tour of your land. Now get some running clothing on and let's go lazy bones."

She jumped to her feet, went to attention and saluted, the shirt opening, baring a shapely right breast.

"Oh my," Rick said. "I might have to alter our uniform for women regulations."

She brought her hand down and slapped him gently on the face with it. Then went to her cupboard and brought out her jogging gear, while Rick pulled on his socks and laced up his combat boots and pulled a light green T shirt over his head.

"Ok ready," she said. "Let's go." After an hour they had completed the tour and she stopped breathlessly leaning on the corral top rail.

"Well hello beauty," Rick said. "What have you got there?"

A brood mare, colt trailing, came up to Tanya and nudged her hand.

"Magda!" Tanya cried, taking the mares head between both her hands and putting her head on her neck. "And who is this fine little man?"

Magda took her head from Tanya's hands and nudged the colt closer. Tanya crouched down and reached through the rails and gently brushed the colt, who skittered away.

"Oh he is beautiful Magda, you did well!"

Magda tossed her head and then trotted away.

"She is my favourite mare," Tanya said. "He was born while we were in Afghanistan this time."

"He has good lines," Rick said. "So does she. I have a stallion she might like."

"Oh," Tanya said. "And does he ride as good as his master?" she said sticking her hand in his pants and squeezing what she found there.

"What?" Rick said, and she took her hand out and ran for the cabin, he right behind her.

After, they lay beside each other. She had her head on his chest and was lazily circling his nipple with her finger.

"When I was sixteen," she said. "My father said he thought it time I found a place where I could be alone. A private place. So I wandered around his property and I found this place. The roof had long since collapsed and the walls were falling down. But it had survived God knows how many winters and revolutions and wars and purges. I could make where an old corral had been and I began to clear the path and the clearing. I took down the old building and had this one put in its place.

"When I was tearing the old building down I found something I have never shown any one. Something special, something precious."

She got up and padded to a dresser, opened a drawer, rummaged around and came back with a board. There was writing on it, faded but still legible. The writing was crylic, but was clearly written with a clean and strong hand.

'Today,' it said. 'October the twelfth eighteen sixty nine, I Andreas Bekenbaum took Elizabeth Helenchuk to be my wife. I will love her forever.'

Beneath that in a female hand was written, 'Today I, Elizabeth Helenchuk, pledge my honour and my life to Andreas Bekenbaum. I will love him forever.'

"I often lay here looking at that board," Tanya said. "Wondering what became of them. What their life was like. Did they end their lives together? Did they love each other to the end?"

"You will just have to come home with me to find out now, won't you?" Rick said.

"But Rick how can we?" she rose on an elbow. "I still have two years left to serve and so do you. I can wait, but it will be hard."

"Well I have had a talk with the Earl," Rick said. "I seem to be one crew short at the moment and I suggested that perhaps we give our Ukrainian brethren a chance to train with us for two years. And guess what, the Earl agreed and told the general to make it happen who told the Colonel to make it happen, who told the Ukrainian colonel to make it happen and so it has come to pass. You and your crew will become my missing crew."

She jumped on him and hugged him.

"When did that happen?" she asked.

"About ten minutes after you accepted my proposal," Rick said. "Colonel von Hoadle, our combat commander, was quite instant on it and of course the Earl had to bow to his advisors and agreed to it."

"Oh my God! I have to contact my troop, they have arrangements to make!" she made to spring off the bed but Rick grabbed her by the waist and held her there.

"They already know don't they?" she said. "You shit." She hit him with both fists.

"This is my sister's engagement present love," Rick said. "She had to use up a lot of favours to make it happen. I kept meaning to tell you, but never found the right moment until now."

"One thing though," Rick said and he pulled his rifle and a clip out from the corner, made sure the clip was loaded and inserted it in the rifle. "You have to be able to put five rounds in the kill zone after running ten klicks in less than two hours. Get your gear love, it's time to go to work."

Chapter Nine

"This people is a C7," Bill said to the assembled group of trainees. "It is not a rifle, it is not an M16, it is not an AK, it is a C7 or a weapon, nothing else. We do not fire our C7 on full automatic. We fire our C7 in semi-automatic two shot groups, is that clear? You will run ten klicks down that path, you will not get lost, you will keep those packs on your back and you will put five rounds into a kill zone target after that ten klick run or you will go back home. Is that clear?"

"Yes Master Warrant!" the group yelled.

Bill held up a stop watch over his head, his hand on the start button and yelled, "Go!"

The group of one hundred and ten trainees took off, Tanya and her group among them. She held her group to a mile eating trot while some of the others, notably the SEALS, took off at a run.

"Would My Lord care for a cool beverage?" Bill asked.

"Why I think My Lord would just," Rick said.

"Don't worry Gadget, she'll do alright, its only ten klicks and they have been training hard."

"I'm not worried," Rick said. "I'm more worried about you and your soft fat ass."

"Ha, that'll be the day I can't run five K and kick some newbie ass."

They finished their beer and shrugged into their well-worn packs, putting their C7s on their shoulders and walked to the tree line bordering the half way mark of the course. There they crouched down out of sight and waited for the trainees to arrive.

They heard them before they saw them. One hundred and ten troopers with heavy loads make a lot of noise. Rick made sure he had his clip of blanks in place and jacked a round into the breach and a flash bang in the grenade launcher. Bill did the same. The groups had tightened up. Tanya's troop was not in the lead, they were in the middle jogging at the same pace. The SEALs were in the lead still but beginning to labour. They were followed as expected by the SAS. Rick shook his head as he saw Whitmore and his Force Recon troop at the rear followed by JTF2.

They waited until the trainees were ten meters down the trail before they stepped out into the middle and let fly with first the flash bangs and then with the five round clips on full auto.

"You fuckers is all dead!" Bill said. "No discipline, Jesus Christ! My five year old kid does better than that!"

He and Rick began to run. As Rick passed the group in the rear he turned around and matched their pace backward while he looked them over and put a full clip in his C7, jacking a round in it and placing it on safety. Then he reloaded another flash bang in the grenade launcher, all without taking his eyes off the running rear enders.

"Not seeing the ambush I could see, nobody does," he said. "The great and oh so wonderful JTF2 being beat by a woman? Shit, now I've seen everything."

Then turning around, he sped up to catch Bill at the head of the group. "Hurry up you slack asses," he said as he passed the middle group. "You'll never make it at this pace."

He and Bill matched the pace of the lead group, gauging it by ear. They kept just far enough ahead to be visible.

"Not bad for a pampered officer," Bill said.

"Ya speak for yourself," Rick said. "I'm not the one with sweat pouring down my face. What are you going to do when it gets hot?"

"Shit I told Pat not to make Pizza for dinner last night, but did she listen. Nooo."

"Well you didn't have to eat it," Rick said.

"Ya right, you try that with your wife after she has spent all day making pizza from scratch."

"They better all pass," Rick said. "We deploy at the end of the week. That doesn't leave them much time to retest."

"Ah shit Rick, a base grunt could pass this run easy."

"It's not the run I'm worried about."

They sprinted the last ten meters and were firing from the standing position when the SAS came into view.

"Come on come on! Get the lead out!" Bill yelled. "You think the Major has all day! I have it on good authority the Major has a hot date with a blond cutie pie tonight and he wants to get out of here!"

That drew some snorts of laughter from Tanya's troop, now in third place.

"What you think that's funny?" Bill said. "I'll show you what's funny when my boot rams up your ass when you can't hit that damn target!"

Rick and Bill strolled up and down the firing line haranguing the troopers constantly. Occasionally firing a round over one's head or a flash bang onto the range.

As expected, SAS finished first clearing weapons and dropping packs at the rest area.

Tanya's troop were firing slow controlled two shot groups from the sitting position as they had been taught and finished in the middle of the pack. The SEALS, as expected were last. Once the firing line was clear, the range officers went down and checked the targets. Everyone had passed.

"OK people," Rick said. "You all passed. One hour fifteen minutes to the last shot, hardly a record. Remember people, you are at altitude here. Your lungs are not used to the lower oxygen levels. Tomorrow you will be moving even higher where you will stay for the next three months. Your first exercise will be to repel an attacking force made up of our raw recruits, kids just out of high school. They won't be joining you for two weeks yet. Make these two weeks count because they could hit you any time after that.

"You won't be joined by the Ukrainian troop. They were just here to pass minimal training requirements and will be joining one of our active duty units as a support and logistics troop. Enjoy the rest of the day and evening people, it will be the last one in civilization for three months"

"Everybody but Major Helenchuk's troop get out of here!" Bill said.

They waited until the trainees were out of site and the range officers joined them. Rick nodded and he and the nine others came up to Tanya's troop and brought two small boxes from their pockets.

Rick fastened first the crossed rifles on Tanya's uniform collar, then the bear. Then he and the rest of the troop took two steps back and saluted.

"You did well today," Rick said. "Better than some of the most elite troops in the world. Welcome to the Bears and Eagles. Because you have already completed basic and advanced infantry training at home and you have all already spent time in a war zone, we can wave the normal requirements for you to receive the bear. Most units in the world would kill to get even that.

"There are only two ways to earn one of these," Rick said touching his eagle. "The first way is to join those other guys in the bush for the next three months and we deploy in three days and we don't have time for that. The other way is to challenge."

"The challenge is done on horseback and includes sabre, lance, pistol and rifle challenges. You may dismount for the rifle and pistol challenge. It is no dishonour not to have an Eagle. My father, the General did not earn his until he was forced to. He kept failing the yearly qualifications on purpose so that other less fortunate people than he could get theirs. I leave it up to you if you would challenge or not. I and every man here will serve with you regardless."

Tanya looked at her people and they all nodded their heads, she marched up to Rick, came to attention and saluted.

"Major! This trooper and her troop would face the challenge sir!"

Rick returned the salute and smiled. "I would expect no less from Blood Cossack and members of Andreas Host. Master Warrant, call down to the stables and have the Riding Master prepare ten Cossack mounts from my string for these troopers. Troopers, you will report to the Riding Master at the stables and you will return here with your mounts. Dismissed."

"This otta be interesting," Bill said. "Your string eh?"

"No sense making it easy on them," Rick said. "I need a beer."

"One of you yahoos, get His Lordship and I a beer." Bill said. "The other yahoos set up the targets."

"Thanks Julia," Rick said. "Grab Pat and a couple of horses, you two can be with the lances."

"Yo Pat," Julia called out. "You're with me, off to the stables we go."

Rick was at the top of the bleachers, his back leaning against the rails, sipping a beer when the riders came in and dismounted. The bleachers were rapidly filling. It wasn't often a challenge was run and rarely with this many challengers. Elizabeth scanned the crowd and found him.

"Hey Liz," Rick said. "Grab a beer."

Elizabeth opened the small cooler and pulled a can from it.

"Those are your ponies aren't they?" she asked. "Do you think that's fair?"

All ten of these horses were Ricks best. They had all been trained as cavalry mounts and were hardly horses for novices.

"Well they call themselves Cossacks and wanted to challenge. It's time they proved it."

"Troopers!" Bill said. "You will challenge this course two at a time. You will ride up over that hill and obtain your lance. You will then come back here and lance the target, then sabre the first and second target, you will proceed to the pistol range and fire five shots. Then to the rifle range where you may dismount and fire ten shots. You must hit every sword and lance target before you enter the firing range. You must hit the kill zone with two pistol shots and five rifle shots. Maximum time allowed is ten minutes. If you go over the time limit, miss any targets or fail the firing range you fail. The rider with the lowest time and best score wins. Nobody plays without handing me five dollars. The winner takes it all and buys the first round. Questions?"

"Yes Master Warrant," Tanya said. "What is the total distance and at what intervals do we leave?"

"Total distance is two kilometres," Bill said. "The following riders do not leave until the preceding riders have both crested the hill and are on their way back down. Anything else?"

"Right then, where's the money?" Bill held out his hand as Julia and Pat spurred their horses down the lane with five lances each.

"Not to worry Major," Bill said as he came up to Tanya who was adjusting her stirrups. "Julia comes from inner city LA and had never seen a horse before and she passed with only two months training. Hell so did I for that matter."

"Thank you for the concern Bill," she said. "But it is not necessary. These are good horses."

"Look," Rick said. "See how she has just shortened the stirrups two notches? Ah and she is making sure the lance scabbard is tight and secure. She's done this before."

The first two troopers took off, not at a gallop but a canter, as did the next two and every pair after until only Tanya and her partner were left. Tanya mounted, making sure the rifle at her back was well placed. Then she repositioned the sword scabbard so it was easy to hand and made sure it was loose in the scabbard. The next thing she did was to remove her pistol and place its cord around her neck before replacing it in the holster. Then she scanned the crowd until she spotted Rick, her partner took off and she stayed, keeping her skittish mount in check, took out her sword kissed the blade and pointed it Rick, smiled and hit the horse on the flank with the side of the blade keeping him to a trot as she scabbarded the sword.

"Ya they've all done this before," Rick said.

"Ya think?" Elizabeth said. Not one had failed yet.

Tanya's partner had started the lance portion of the course while Tanya was just half way down the hill and she spurred her horse to a gallop. He had finished the firing range as she approached the pistol range at full gallop and fired off her five rounds letting the pistol drop and flipping the rifle off her back she fired a fast five rounds then deftly flipped backwards and fired another five as she rode away. Then she flipped the rifle back on her back and reined the horse in sharply spinning him around while holstering her pistol and she spurred him back down the line flipping completely under and back up to the saddle, then hooked her left leg around the saddle horn and flopped over the side grabbing a fallen bottle from the ground as she sped by. The crowd went nuts.

Rick anxiously watched the range officer and sighed a big sigh of relief when he signalled pass. By this time Tanya was once again before the centre of the bleachers. Once again this time with a wink and a big grin, she withdrew her sword, kissed it and pointed it at Rick. She put it back in place, turned her horse and walked away. At the last moment she turned to look back at Rick, stuck her tongue out, flipped her hair and galloped away.

"I think I will let my mare meet your stallion," Tanya said in her sweet accented English, later laying on top of Rick. "He rides almost as good as his master."

"Ya ya, rub it in," Rick said.

"Well it serves you right for not telling me you had arranged for us to come here," she said. "You are not too upset with me?"

"No, not at all," Rick said. "You are almost as good as Liz. Now before we can let your mare meet my stallion. I have to see how good a ride her master is."

Tanya giggled as Rick flipped her on her back and found out.

She had hoped to spend a lazy morning together. It was their last day. Tomorrow they would board an aircraft to spend the next three months in Afghanistan. Rick was already up and he was dressing, not in his normal blue jeans and T shirt, but dark slacks and a light cotton shirt. He was fresh shaved and was combing his hair. She sighed and knew he had something else in mind. When she came out of the shower, he was nowhere to be seen, but had left a note telling her he would be right back and to dress nice.

She chose a nice skirt and tasteful blouse and was brushing her long blond hair in preparation for braiding it when he walked in, two bunches of lilies in hand. He dropped the flowers on the table and came to her, kissing her on the top of her head.

"Leave it loose," he said. "I want them to see you with your beautiful hair down and free. Put on some walking shoes, we have about a kilometre to go to meet them."

Tanya was still puzzled as he handed her one of the bunches of lilies and they walked out of the yard in a new direction. He did not speak as he walked and he seemed withdrawn, so she let him be, content to be holding his hand as they walked and listening to the sounds of nature as the busy ranch noises fell behind them. They soon came to a path that disappeared into the trees and he turned down it and it opened up into a beautifully kept grave yard in a clearing surrounded by large pine trees. There were not many graves here and she knew it was the family plot.

He stopped first in front of two large graves set apart from the others. Both grave stones had bronze reliefs on them depicting horses in full flight.

"The one on the left is Bartholomew. He was Andreas' horse. It is said he saved Andreas' life three times in battle. The other is Lady, Elizabeth's mare. They both are the root of our blood lines and were much loved by Andreas and Elizabeth."

He took her next to a newer pair of grave stones, one had the depiction of a Victoria Cross on it, the other the old Russian imperil eagle. "This is my great grandfather John and his wife Tatiana. They were both heroes in their own right. He won the Victoria Cross in the First World War and she is responsible for many of our business successes outside of the oil and gas industry."

Tanya wondered where she had seen the inscription beneath the Imperial Eagle on Tatiana's head stone but she could not recall and did not want to ask.

"You said to me that you often wondered about Andreas and Elizabeth, what became of them and did they live their lives in love to the end? Here is Andreas and Elizabeth."

The stones were large and inscribed in German and Russian. They listed all of their awards and titles. Rick placed his bunch of lilies at Andreas' head stone and knelt down and made the sign of the cross, bowing his head in prayer. Tanya placed hers at Elizabeth's head stone and followed Rick in prayer. After short time he stood and helped her up, putting his arm around her.

"They lived their full lives together Tanya." Rick said. "The whole time they were never apart. They both fought in Afghanistan, together. They trekked across North America together and they established this settlement together. They lived long enough to see it prosper. Andreas had ridden out with his grandchildren to go fishing and they came across an old large grizzly bear who charged them. He sent the kids back home and charged the bear shooting it six times in the chest with his Colt. The bear died, but not before it got him. Elizabeth came to him and he died in her arms after making sure the kids were alright and making a final joke with her. Five days after they buried him, they found her dead in her bed laying face up with a smile on her face."

"Andreas, Elizabeth, I am Richard, son of Paul, son of Nicolas, son of John, son of Andreas, house of Bekebaum," Rick said softly in German.

"This is Tanya, house of Helenchuk. She lives on the land where you spent your wedding night and found your words of everlasting love and she cherishes them as did you. I love her as much as you loved each other and she is to be my wife. Bless us."

"Andreas, Elizabeth," Tanya said in Russian. "I am Tanya, daughter of Sonya, house of Helenchuk. I love Richard with all my heart and all my soul and will try hard to be as you were together all your lives. I ask you to bless us and watch over us."

"I am Nicolas, your grandson. I too ask you to bless this union." Nicolas said.

"I am Katherine, daughter of Tatiana, daughter of Elizabeth, I approve of this match and ask your blessing."

Tanya turned around to see Rick hugging his grandparents who were still kneeling as were his father and mother. All of them were crying and she felt the tears well up in her eyes and Elizabeth came to her and hugged her, tears running down her cheeks.

"This is the first time he has been here since he was a little boy and then it was only because he was forced to," Elizabeth said. "Do you know how special this is, that he has done this on his own? That he brought you here, to this place?"

"Tatiana always said there is no such thing as coincidence," Katherine said, walking over and stroking her headstone. "Andreas rescued Elizabeth and her sister Katia from bandits. Their father's last name was Helenchuk. They spent their first night together as man and wife in a cabin and you found their profession of enduring love and kept it. You and Richard found each other in Afghanistan and never having seen each other before or knowing each other's names, you fell in love. He rescues you, not knowing you were there on the same battlefield that Andreas and Elizabeth fought on. No this was no coincidence, this was God's work. God, Andreas and Elizabeth made this happen. They have already blessed this union."

The next day, Rick and Tanya were asleep, her head on his shoulder as they flew to Afghanistan.

Authors Notes

On September 11, 2001, 2000 people, 24 of them Canadian were killed in the attacks in the U.S.A. carried out that day.

The first response of Canada and her people, were to host the thousands of stranded air travellers who had no place to land after the United States closed the airspace in the country. The second, was to guarantee supplies of crude oil at a set price to the U.S.A.

In early October, Joint Task Force 2, JTF2, was deployed to Afghanistan, without the knowledge of the Canadian Prime Minister or Cabinet. In late 2001, 40 members of JTF2 were deployed as members of Task Force K-Bar in Afghanistan. Again, the Prime Minister had not been informed, but the Defence Minister had been.

Early in 2002, members of the third battalion Princess Patricias Canadian Light Infantry, PPCLI 3, were deployed alongside US Army airborne troops to search and destroy Al Qaeda infrastructure and commands.

News footage of the first Royal Canadian Airforce transport plane arriving in Afghanistan was shown on Canadian television stations. The first four soldiers off of the aircraft were not high ranking officers. They were four soldiers in combat gear. Two of them carrying encased long rifles on their shoulders. These four soldiers were hurriedly escorted to a waiting HMVV with US Marine markings on it and driven away. Several days later, long standing long range sniper kill records were broken by *US Marines.*

The first 3 LAVIII surveillance vehicles in Afghanistan, were also hurriedly dispatched to Kandahar Province and the vehicles and troopers attached to the US Marines. These LAVIIIs are virtually identical to the LAV25s the US Marines operate, but with proprietary electronic surveillance suites installed.

After decades of neglect, the Canadian Armed Forces were required to operate in an environment which their basic equipment was not designed for. PPCLI 3 members, were required to *liberate,* tan paint to paint their vehicles from the normal green camouflage paint scheme, to tan. It was also not unheard of for them to also paint their uniforms.

When asked about this, the Canadian Prime Minister made a joke saying that at least we would not be seen at night in the dark green uniforms. The public back lash at this joke was immediate and strong.

It did not help things, when a short time later the first combat deaths since the Korean Conflict occurred. Conducting an approved night training exercise, in an approved exercise area, a US Airforce F16 pilot, despite being told and ordered not to, dropped a 500lb bomb. Four members of PPCLI 3 were killed and 14 wounded.

At the time of first deployment, the Canadian Forces were an integrated command. All the branches of the military shared equipment and uniforms. Members of the individual branches could and did, transfer among the branches and in fact were encouraged to do so. I personally witnessed naval personal manning a water treatment plant at Canadian Forces Base Suffield, which is located in the prairie lands of Alberta, thousands of kilometres from any oceans. At CFB Cold Lake, an airforce base, I was escorted around the base by a Master Corporal from PPCLI 1. He and nine more members of the same unit, were cross training with the airforce. The Master Corporal only had a few years left until retirement and he had made the wise choice to be trained as an air conditioning technician. A trade that is lucrative in civilian life as well as military life.

The normal procedure went something like this. The ten PPCLI 1 troopers, were still on the PPCLI books as active members. They were also classed as active members of 4 Wing Cold Lake by the airforce. So in the convoluted government accounting methods, those ten soldiers were made to look like twenty, while only paying for ten.

Of the eventual 3000 troops on duty in Kandahar Province at the height of Canadian occupation of the area, only 1000 were classed as combat troops. Generally there were only 800 deployed in the field. Of those, roughly 2/3rds were part time reserve soldiers. These reservists were highly trained and highly motivated.

The Calgary Highlanders, the Kings Own (Calgary) Regiment, along with other Alberta Reserve battalions made large contributions of young troopers. The Calgary Highlanders in particular with the highest level of participation of any other reserve battalion with 110 deployments. KOCR was right behind them, also over 100.

To the laymen, there will be no difference. The soldiers of these units were slotted into the vacant spots of the Regular Forces, Reg Force, units. PPCLI 1, 2, 3. Royal Canadian Rifles, RCR 1, 2, 3. Royal 22, Vandoos, 1, 2, 3. Lord Strathcona Horse (Royal Canadians) in the main.

At the same time, the professional officer corps had to transition from the old Peace Keeping model, to the new aggressive role they now had to master. Not all transitioned well. Many were just there to obtain the 180 day minimum in a war zone to advance their careers and were not suited for combat roles. And it showed.

Added to the fact was that the bad guys came out of Pakistan, who was supposed to be an ally. Once the bad guys ran out of supplies or men, they ran back across the border and safety. NATO troops were not allowed to pursue them. The war was basically being conducted the same way the Vietnam War was conducted. With the same results.

Eventually, Canadian long suffering troops were provided with modern up to date equipment, uniforms and weapon systems. The government was voted out and the new government separated the contingents in the Canadian Armed Forces, back to their original roles and designations. Army, Navy and Airforce. The Royal Canadian Army. The Royal Canadian Navy, RCN. The Royal Canadian Airforce, RCAF. They were allowed to revert back to their original ranks, uniforms, unit designations and traditions.

Asking ourselves why we were still in Afghanistan ten years later with no signs of change. Canada, along with other NATO signatory countries, ended our involvement in Afghanistan. 159 of our sons and daughters were killed and another 1859 were wounded. 40,000 troops served in total. $18 billion were spent.

To our governments credit, they did not succumb to pressure from the U.S. or Britain to commit more boots on the ground. Our people accomplished just as much as the much larger U.S. contingents did before we arrived and after we left, with the same results and higher casualties.

Don't miss out!

Click the button below and you can sign up to receive emails whenever R.P. Wollbaum publishes a new book. There's no charge and no obligation.

https://books2read.com/r/B-A-DWJC-AJWT

Connecting independent readers to independent writers.

Also by R.P. Wollbaum

Baren und Adler
Baren und Adler

Bears and Eagles
Bears and Eagles
Eagles Claw
Eagle's Talon
As Eagles Swarm
Bears Maul
Desert Eagle
Eagle's Nest

Wind Riders
Oaken

Watch for more at www.bearsandeagles.com.